TOEFL
托福字彙 上冊

李英松／著

［2500托福字彙 ＋相似詞補充＋詞性連結］

輕鬆舉一反三，
有效擴展你的英語字庫！

e of pottery.　　　An ominous view would be threatening.
陶器)　　　不祥的（形容詞）

atening.　悲傷地(副詞)　To speak ruefully means to speak sorrowfully.
　　　　　　Dresden is a type of pottery.　An or
us task is one which is burdensome.　陶器(名詞，德國陶器)　繁重的

容詞)　An epigram is a witty thought.　　　　　　To exemplify means
ting.　警語，思想(名詞)　A parody is an imitation.　例示(不定詞)
　　　　　　模仿(名詞)
rs to sarcasm.　　　　To be impeccable is to be blameless.
) A valid story is sound.　無瑕疵的，完善的 (形容詞)

確實的 (形容詞)　To affiliate with a group is to join it.　To mesmerize persons is to h
　　　　結交，聯絡 (不定詞)　迷惑(不定詞)

e who is lazy.　　　　　　　　　　　　　An indo
n refers to unity.　An insolent manner is insulting.　A love potion is a disease.　懶惰的(
　　　無禮的，侮慢的 (形容詞)　劑藥(隱) (名詞)
)　　　　　　　　　　　　　　　　To be indicted means
A tithe is given to a government.　控告 (動詞，被動式)
交稅 (名詞)　A vocation is a job.　When you corroborate a sto
　　　　　職業 (名詞)　確定 (動詞)　A person who is fa
e is a trace. Egotists think of themselves.　好開玩笑的(形容詞
詞)　自私 (名詞)
　　　　An insolent manner is insulting.　An antid
subscription.　無禮的，侮慢的 (形容詞)　對策，認

An anthropologist is one who studies the human race.

自
序

　　我們都知道，不管是學習本國語文，還是學習外國語文，多從單字開始，之後才是成語、短句、長句、段落，最後成為文章。我們也知道，要記住單字何其困難，尤其是對於文字不是英文字母組合而成的各國國民而言，更是難上加難。

　　當今世界上，最通用的語文非美國式英語文莫屬（英國式英語文在某些拼字或者讀音上有些不同，但不構成我們學習上的障礙，讀者大可不必在意）。因此，學習美國式英語文就成為我們必需修的課題。無論在學校求學中，或者是在社會上求職就業，都要經歷過英語文的考試。又有誰知道，你我當中，有多少人在紅字邊緣，有些人甚至被當掉。無可否認，有極少數的人，對學習語文的能力真是驚人，可說是天才，然而對絕大多數的人而言，確實讓人頭疼。

　　一般公認，學習一國的語文，從簡而難 可分為聽、說、讀和寫四個階段。旅美期間，與美國人交談，不管是白人，還是黑人，有時候關鍵字(key word)搞不清楚是哪個字，要求他寫出來時，往往無法拼出正確的字。此時此刻，讓筆者想起童年時代，暑假農忙時期，要幫忙父母做些農事，有位姑丈問筆者，鋤頭和筆哪一樣比較重？筆者毫不加以考慮，答曰鋤頭當然比較重。那位長輩居然笑笑地解釋道，拿起筆來，遲遲無法寫出一個字來，有如千斤重擔，而提起鋤頭挖土，卻是輕鬆自在。筆者當時年少無法知其真義，直至年歲漸長，方知其道理之所在。

　　很多人想要增進自己的英語文程度，以便出國留學或者進入社會工作，往往無法達成自己的期許，遭遇挫折，氣餒油然而生。筆者是過來人深知箇中滋味，因而腦海中浮現了一個念頭，何不將多年來所收集的資料整理成書，以饗讀者。本書之內容有三大特點：

第一，打破傳統，不按照英文字母的順序，而以收集資料的先後編著。其理由在於逼迫讀者不斷地翻看字典，進而刺激大腦不會產生倦怠與枯燥感。

第二，從完整的英文句子中先記住單字 其目的在於，我們完全了解句子的前後文意義之後，要記住單字當可事半而功倍，並且不容易忘記。

第三，本書不但將單字翻成中文，列出一個相似字之外，還將其詞類寫出來， 方便讀者能夠舉一反三，從翻查英英字典或者英漢字典之中，找出更多的相似字，以及它們的詞類（諸如，動詞、副詞、形容詞、名詞之類）。

　　最後，以簡短的兩句英文，與讀者們共勉之「Just Do It.」「Don't Worry. Be Happy.」同時要感謝姪女李昭儀對本書的校對、印刷及姪子李鍊賦的排版與設計，他們在百忙之中，讓本書予以出版，功不可沒。當然，讀者在研讀之後，英語文的聽、說、讀和寫之能力，得以精進，是為作者之殷殷期盼！

TOEFL

托福字彙

1. An **ominous** view would be **threatening**.

    註解　不祥的 (形容詞)

2. To speak **ruefully** means to speak **sorrowfully.**

    註解　悲傷地(副詞)

3. To **mesmerize** persons is to **hypnotize** them.

    註解　迷惑(不定詞)

4. An **onerous** task is one which is **burdensome**.

    註解　繁重的(形容詞)

5. A **valid** story is **sound**.

    註解　確實的 (形容詞)

6. An **epigram** is a witty **thought**.

    註解　警語，思想(名詞)

7. **Dresden** is a type of **pottery**.

    註解　陶器(名詞，德國陶器)

8. To **exemplify** means to **illustrate**.

    註解　例示(不定詞)

9. A **rendezvous** is a **meeting-place**.

    註解　會合地(名詞)

10. A **raucous** sound is **hoarse**.

    註解　沙啞的(形容詞)

11. An **indolent** man is one who is **lazy**.

    註解　懶惰的(形容詞)

12. **Irony** refers to **sarcasm**.

    註解　諷刺(名詞)

13. A **parody** is an **imitation**.

    註解　模仿(名詞)

14. An act which is **tantamount** to guilt is **equal to it**.

    註解　相等的(形容詞)

15. A **stigma** refers to **a mark of disgrace**.

    註解　汙名，瑕疵(名詞)

16. **Forensic** refers to **debates**.

    註解　辯論(名詞)

17. **Tangible** evidence is **perceptible**.

    註解　確實的，可以認知的(形容詞)

18. To **paraphrase** a statement is to **restate it**.
   > 註解　重述(不定詞)

19. A **transient** meeting is **fleeting**.
   > 註解　短暫的(形容詞)

20. **Progeny** is **offspring**.
   > 註解　子孫，結果(名詞)

21. Snakes that are **innocuous** are **harmless**.
   > 註解　無毒的，無害的(形容詞)

22. The **veracity** of a person's statement refers to the statement's **truthfulness**.
   > 註解　確實，坦白(名詞)

23. A **prodigious** meal is **enormous**.
   > 註解　巨大的(形容詞)

24. An **enervating** climate would be a climate that **weakens** you.
   > 註解　無力的(形容詞，同義字為動詞)

25. A **lyre** is a musical **instrument**.
   > 註解　七弦琴，樂器(名詞)

26. An **amulet** is **a lucky charm**.
   > 註解　護身符(名詞)

27. **Filial** love is love of **children for parents**.
   > 註解　子女的，孝順的(形容詞)

28. **Marital** feeling exists between **married** persons.
   > 註解　戰爭的，結婚的(形容詞)

29. A **profusion** of products implies **abundance**.
   > 註解　很多，豐富(名詞)

30. To **promulgate** the truth means to **publish it**.
   > 註解　公佈，傳播(不定詞)

31. **Discretion** which is the better part of valor refers to **caution**.
   > 註解　謹慎(名詞)

32. To **elicit** means to **draw out**.
   > 註解　抽出(不定詞)

33. A **discriminating** person notes what **different** is.
   > 註解　有辨識力的，區別的(形容詞)

34. A **derelict** is an **outcast**.

   註解　被遺棄的人或物(名詞)

35. **Nefarious** schemes are **wicked**.

   註解　兇惡的(形容詞)

36. A **morbid** story is **gloomy**.

   註解　不健康的，悲觀的(形容詞)

37. An **indomitable** spirit is **unconquerable**.

   註解　不能征服的(形容詞)

38. **Denizens** of a city are **citizens**.

   註解　居民，公民(名詞)

39. A **zenith** refers to a **summit**.

   註解　巔峰，最高點(名詞)

40. **Calloused** feelings are **hardened**.

   註解　無情的，堅硬的(形容詞)

41. To award a medal **posthumously** means to award it **after death**.

   註解　死後的(形容詞)

42. To **improvise** a fancy costume is to **make it without much preparation**.

   註解　即席而作 (不定詞)

43. To **epitomize** is to **summarize**.

   註解　摘要(不定詞)

44. A **cosmopolitan** person is **worldly**.

   註解　四海爲家的(形容詞)

45. An **obituary** column deals with **deaths**.

   註解　訃文(名詞)

46. A **flamboyant** personality is **virtuous**.

   註解　燦爛的(形容詞)

47. A **didactic** occupation would require **teaching**.

   註解　教誨的(形容詞)

48. A **mendicant** is a **beggar**.

   註解　乞丐(名詞)

49. **Diverse** items are **varied**.

   註解　種種的，形形色色的(形容詞)

50. **Rehabilitated** criminals are **restored**.

   註解　修復的，改造的(形容詞)

51. A **sinecure** is a position which requires **little work**.
    註解 閒差(名詞)

52. To be **implacable** is to be **perplexed**.
    註解 難解的 (形容詞)

53. An **adage** refers to a **proverb**.
    註解 格言(名詞)

54. An **odyssey** is a **long journey**.
    註解 長期的冒險旅行(名詞)

55. **Dulcet** tones are **pleasant**.
    註解 悅耳的(形容詞)

56. An **analogy** is a **comparison**.
    註解 類似 (名詞)

57. A **modicum** of gory is a **small mount**.
    註解 少量 (名詞)

58. An **incongruity** is an **inconsistency**.
    註解 不相稱，前後不一致 (名詞)

59. A **reprehensible** neglect of duty would be **blamable**.
    註解 應受責難的 (形容詞)

60. To note **discrepancies** to note **differences**.
    註解 不同，矛盾 (名詞)

61. A **callow** youth is one who is **inexperienced**.
    註解 沒有經驗的 (形容詞)

62. An **oboe** is a **wind instrument**.
    註解 雙簧管樂器 (名詞)

63. An **obnoxious** person is **unpopular**.
    註解 使人討厭的 (形容詞)

64. To **obfuscate** means to **obscure**.
    註解 使模糊 (不定詞)

65. **Hypochondriacs** are people who think they are **sick**.
    註解 憂鬱症，臆想病 (名詞)

66. **Beguiling** river byways are **bewitching**.
    註解 令人陶醉的 (形容詞)

67. **Rattan** is a type of **reed**.
    註解 藤條，蘆葦 (名詞)

68. A **gourmet** is fond of **food**.

   註解　美食的人 (名詞)

69. **Cerebral** pertains to the **brain**.

   註解　大腦 (名詞)

70. A **transitory** feeling is **fleeting**.

   註解　短暫的 (形容詞)

71. A feeling of **animosity** is one of **hatred**.

   註解　仇恨 (名詞)

72. An **allegory** is a **fable**.

   註解　寓言，傳說 (名詞)

73. A person **ostracized** by society is **barred**.

   註解　排斥的 (形容詞)

74. Boiling **cauldrons** are **dishes**.

   註解　鍋，碟，盤 (名詞，亦同 caldrons)

75. To **subsidize** means to **give financial aid**.

   註解　金錢支助 (不定詞)

76. An **insurrection** is an **uprising**.

   註解　暴動 (名詞)

77. When a country **capitulates**, it **surrenders**.

   註解　投降 (動詞)

78. To be **naive** is to be **unaffected**.

   註解　天真的 (形容詞)

79. **Dogmatic** views are **positive**.

   註解　教理的，武斷的 (形容詞)

80. **Edification** refers to **instruction**.

   註解　啟迪，教化 (名詞)

81. A **paragon** is a **model**.

   註解　模範 (名詞)

82. A **grotesque** figure is **ridiculous**.

   註解　古怪的，可笑的 (形容詞)

83. To **defer** payment means to **put it off**.

   註解　延緩 (不定詞)

84. An **elegy** is a **funeral song**.

   註解　輓歌 (名詞)

85. **Debauchery** refers to **drunkenness**.
註解 放蕩，酗酒 (名詞)

86. **Initiative** refers to **self-reliance**.
註解 主動 (名詞)

87. A **vestige** is a **trace**.
註解 痕跡 (名詞)

88. An **anthropologist** is one who studies **the human race**.
註解 人類學家 (名詞)

89. An **insolent** manner is **insulting**.
註解 無禮的，侮慢的 (形容詞)

90. **An antidote** refers to **a subscription**.
註解 對策，認捐 (名詞)

91. A person who is **facetious** is **happy**.
註解 好開玩笑的 (形容詞)

92. **Egotists** think of **themselves**.
註解 自私 (名詞)

93. A **vocation** is a **job**.
註解 職業 (名詞)

94. When you **corroborate** a statement, you **confirm** it.
註解 確定 (動詞)

95. To be **indicted** means to be **charged**.
註解 控告 (動詞，被動式)

96. To **affiliate** with a group is to **join it**.
註解 結交，聯絡 (不定詞)

97. A **tithe** is given to a **government**.
註解 交稅 (名詞)

98. **Cohesion** refers to **unity**.
註解 團結 (名詞)

99. A love **potion** is **a disease**.
註解 一劑藥(隱) (名詞)

100. To be **impeccable** is to be **blameless**.
註解 無瑕疵的，完善的 (形容詞)

101. A **furtive** glance would be **sly**.
註解 狡猾的 (形容詞)

102. An **enigma** is a **riddle**.

    > 註解　謎，難解的人或事 (名詞)

103. **Culinary** habits pertain to the **kitchen**.

    > 註解　廚房的，烹調的 (形容詞)

104. A **pessimistic** view is usually **gloomy**.

    > 註解　悲觀者的 (形容詞)

105. A judge who is **meticulous** is **scrupulous**.

    > 註解　拘泥細節的，過多考慮的 (形容詞)

106. To be in a state of **lethargy** is to be **ill**.

    > 註解　昏睡，倦怠 (名詞)

107. A **scalawag** (or scallywag) is a **rascal**.

    > 註解　流氓，惡棍 (名詞)

108. **Choreography** applies to the field of **dance**.

    > 註解　舞蹈 (名詞)

109. **Obesity** refers to **fatness**.

    > 註解　肥胖 (名詞)

110. **Sedentary** work is **stationary**.

    > 註解　久坐的，不動的 (形容詞)

111. A **dirge** is a **funeral hymn**.

    > 註解　喪曲，輓歌 (名詞)

112. An **exonerated** prisoner is one who has been **paroled**.

    > 註解　免罪的，假釋的 (形容詞)

113. To **abrogate** a treaty means to **abolish it**.

    > 註解　廢止 (不定詞)

114. A **prosaic** book is one that is **unimaginative**.

    > 註解　平淡的，缺乏想像力的 (形容詞)

115. **Damask** refers to **coarse material**.

    > 註解　斜紋布，粗糙的料 (名詞)

116. A **voracious** person is **greedy**.

    > 註解　貪婪的 (形容詞)

117. To be **cumbersome** means to be **clumsy**.

    > 註解　阻礙，拖累，笨拙的 (形容詞)

118. An **agnostic** is a **disbeliever**.

    > 註解　不可知論者，不信者 (名詞)

119. To **rejuvenate** means to **renew**.

   註解　使恢復活力 (不定詞)

120. A **palatable** food is **delicious**.

   註解　味美的 (形容詞)

121. A **la carte** on a menu indicates **each item separately priced**.

   註解　分別標價 (名詞，羅馬字)

122. An **impetuous** act is one which is **rash**.

   註解　輕率的 (形容詞)

123. A **clandestine** meeting is **secret**.

   註解　祕密的 (形容詞)

124. A woman's **prerogative** is her **privilege**.

   註解　特權 (名詞)

125. When two parties **parley**, they attend a **conference**.

   註解　談判，商議 (動詞，同義字爲名詞)

126. A **droll** character is one that is **amusing**.

   註解　滑稽的 (形容詞)

127. A speech which is **impromptu** is **without preparation**.

   註解　臨時的，事先未準備的 (形容詞)

128. A woman's **intuition** is often **instinctive**.

   註解　直覺，第六感 (名詞，同義字爲形容詞)

129. **Avid** is not the same as arid, for avid means **eager**.

   註解　熱望的 (形容詞)

130. An **itinerary** is **plan of a journey**.

   註解　旅行計劃 (名詞)

131. The actress traveling **incognito** travels **under an assumed name.**

   註解　隱姓埋名地 (副詞)

132. **Copious** tears are **plentiful**.

   註解　豐富的 (形容詞)

133. The **Hippocratic** oath is taken by **doctors**.

   註解　古希臘醫生的 (形容詞，引用現代醫生的誓約)

134. A **virile** person is **manly**.

   註解　男性的，剛健的 (形容詞)

135. The **picador** performs in a **bullfight**.

   註解　騎馬鬥牛士 (名詞)

136. **Therapy** is **treatment**.
     註解　治療 (名詞)

137. **Consommé** is a **meat**.
     註解　清燉肉湯 (名詞，法國語)

138. **Capricious** people are **changeable**.
     註解　反覆無常的 (形容詞)

139. A **prerequisite** for a course is a **requirement**.
     註解　必須，必要條件 (名詞)

140. People who are **mercenary** think of **money**.
     註解　傭兵，雇來的人 (名詞)

141. A face which is **livid** is **pale**.
     註解　土色的，蒼白的 (形容詞)

142. An **insidious** politician is **treacherous**.
     註解　陰險的，不忠的 (形容詞)

143. To be **explicit** means to be **definite**.
     註解　直爽的，明白的 (形容詞)

144. To be **inundated** s to be **flooded**.
     註解　淹沒的 (形容詞)

145. An **adroit** move is **skillful**.
     註解　機巧的 (形容詞)

146. A **maudlin** person is **sentimental**.
     註解　易傷感的 (形容詞)

147. A famous **Stradivarius** refers to a **violin**.
     註解　小提琴 (名詞，原爲義大利小提琴家之名)

148. A **reminiscence** is a **reminder**.
     註解　回憶 (名詞)

149. A **culmination** of ideas is a **summit**.
     註解　最頂點 (名詞)

150. A **sexagenarian** is between the ages of **sixty to seventy**.
     註解　六十歲至七十歲的人 (名詞)

151. **Claustrophobia** is the fear of being **sick**.
     註解　幽閉恐懼症 (名詞，同義字爲形容詞)

152. **Esthetic** views pertain to **beauty**.
     註解　美的 (形容詞，同 aesthetic)

153. **Cynical** people are **distrustful**.
     > 註解　懷疑人生之價值的 (形容詞)

154. A **mendacious** person is a **liar**.
     > 註解　不誠實的 (形容詞，同義字為名詞)

155. A **cursory** examination would be **hasty**.
     > 註解　粗略的 (形容詞)

156. When you **initiate** something, you **start** it.
     > 註解　創始，開始 (動詞)

157. To **revoke** a license is to **repeal** it.
     > 註解　廢止，取消 (不定詞)

158. A **chronoscope** measures time **intervals**.
     > 註解　計時器，時間距離 (名詞)

159. A **conventional** act is **customary**.
     > 註解　傳統的，習慣的 (形容詞)

160. An **impresario** is a **janitor**.
     > 註解　守衛，管理人 (名詞)

161. **Rancor** is **hatred**.
     > 註解　仇恨 (名詞)

162. The **disintegration** of an area is its **breaking up**.
     > 註解　分解，崩潰 (名詞)

163. A **somnambulist** is **sleepwalker**.
     > 註解　夢遊者 (名詞)

164. A **nostalgia** feeling is **melancholy**.
     > 註解　思鄉病，鄉愁，沉思 (名詞)

165. To be **oblivious** of the truth is to be **forgetful**.
     > 註解　忘記的 (形容詞)

166. To be **reciprocated** is to be **exchanged**.
     > 註解　回報的，互換的 (形容詞)

167. **Voluminous** garments are **full**.
     > 註解　多產的，龐大的 (形容詞)

168. An **ostensible** object is **apparent**.
     > 註解　外表的，明顯的 (形容詞)

169. **Preposterous** songs are **absurd**.
     > 註解　反常的，荒謬的 (形容詞)

170. A **prodigal** is **wasteful**.

    | 註解 | 浪費的 (形容詞)

171. A **laconic** statement is **clear**.

    | 註解 | 簡明的 (形容詞)

172. A **cantankerous** person is **ill-tempered**.

    | 註解 | 難相處的，壞脾氣的 (形容詞)

173. To write an **epistle** is to write a **letter**.

    | 註解 | 書信 (名詞)

174. A **kleptomaniac** has an irresistible urge to **steal**.

    | 註解 | 有竊盜狂的人 (名詞，同義字為不定詞)

175. **Strategic** positions are **fortified**.

    | 註解 | 戰略上的，設防的 (形容詞，同 strategical)

176. Mr. Lee is threatening to go to court to prove that he did not receive an **equitable** (impartial) share of the property.

    | 註解 | 公平的 (形容詞)

177. **Partisan** (Biased) politics is practiced to a very great extent in our government.

    | 註解 | 同黨的，有偏見的 (形容詞)

178. Senator Moore's **partisanship** (inequity) toward industrial and business interests is clearly reflected in his decision to vote against the pollution control bill.

    | 註解 | 黨派意識，不公正 (名詞)

179. As winter drew nears the squirrels hurried to **cache** (hide) away nuts to eat during the long, cold months ahead.

    | 註解 | 隱藏 (不定詞)

180. **Nettled** (Irritated) by pesky mosquitoes, we left the swampy are quickly and continued our hike on higher ground.

    | 註解 | 惹怒 (過去分詞)

181. Mariane's lack of attentiveness **vexed** (annoyed) her teacher, who was attempting to explain the uses of correlative conjunctions to the class.

    | 註解 | 使惱火 (動詞)

182. As I entered the small country church, I was aware of the **stark** (desolate), unadorned interior.

    | 註解 | 純然的，荒涼的 (形容詞)

183. Looking like a young aristocrat, the smiling bride swept **regally** (royally) down the aisle and joined her nervous groom at the altar.

   註解　款待地，盛大地 (副詞)

184. The detective discovered that a lethal **potion** (dose) had been added to the dead man's coffee.

   註解　一服，一劑 (名詞)

185. **Hybridism** (Crossbred) has produced animals of unusual stamina.

   註解　混種，雜交 (名詞)

186. Mr. Staples is **munificent** (generous) in his praise, while Miss Brown hardly ever even acknowledges that you've done something right.

   註解　慷慨的，寬厚的 (形容詞)

187. My grandfather, a **benign** (kind) old gentleman, always greeted us with a gentle smile and slipped us a handful candy.

   註解　親切的 (形容詞)

188. Because Warner's is so **dilatory** (tending to delay) in filling orders, many customers are taking their business to stores that are more prompt.

   註解　拖延的 (形容詞)

189. The American Medical Association recently uncovered the operations of a **charlatan** (someone who pretends to have a skill does not possess) in New York who had been charging ten thousand dollars for his so-called "cure" for cancer.

   註解　走江湖者，庸醫 (名詞)

190. Most foreigners consider the average American to be materialistic and **bumptious** (arrogant), interested on in what benefits him and eager to prove the rest of world how superior he is.

   註解　傲慢的 (形容詞)

191. A saline solution is easily made since water is a **solvent** (dissolved) for salt.

   註解　能溶解的 (形容詞)

192. The hunters **ravaged** (pillaged) the enemy's village to avenge the death of their chief.

   註解　毀掉，掠奪 (動詞)

193. In the early part of the twentieth century the most popular **mode** (style) of transportation was the railroad.

> 註解 方式，風尚 (名詞)

194. The salesman's sudden disappearance **spawned** (generated) many ugly rumors about his personal life.

> 註解 產生，生育 (動詞)

195. The dancers at the party gyrated and **writhed** (distorted) to the pulsating rhythm of the music.

> 註解 扭動 (動詞)

196. Charles spoke to his mother so **peevishly** (contrarily) when she would not let him have the car that she in turn became insane.

> 註解 易怒地，抱怨地 (副詞)

197. The **pauper** (beggar) was so destitute that he did not have enough money for a pair of shoes.

> 註解 乞丐，窮人 (名詞)

198. On welfare rolls there are many who are **destitute** (deprived) because they are physically unable to earn a living.

> 註解 窮困的 (形容詞)

199. Being expelled from school can **stigmatize** (tarnish) your entire life, making it hard to get the kind of job you want.

> 註解 指責，玷污 (動詞)

200. The twentieth Amendment to the Constitution ratified in 1933 set January 20th as the day of **inauguration** (installment).

> 註解 就職典禮 (名詞)

201. Sarah keeps her room in **deplorable** (lamentable) condition shoes, skirts, blouses, papers, books and empty boxes are strewn about everywhere.

> 註解 可嘆的，可悲的 (形容詞)

202. The young father spoke **imploringly** (entreatingly) as he sought help from the welfare agency for his hungry children.

> 註解 哀求地，苦求地 (副詞)

203. The two policemen **dauntlessly** (dismayedly) pursued the escaping convict even though he was firing at them as he ran.

> 註解 無助地，驚慌地 (副詞)

204. Prejudice **impairs** (hinders) our ability to deal fairly with people who are different from ourselves.

    註解　削弱，妨礙 (動詞)

205. The newspaper editorial about the derelict automobiles left to decay in junkyards was really a **satire** (irony) on the incompetence of the city government.

    註解　諷刺 (名詞)

206. Although Mr. Davis was often asked to speak to school groups about his experience in the war, he consistently **declined** (deteriorated) to do so.

    註解　謝絕 (動詞)

207. The teacher asked the students to turn in their work promptly so that he would not be **deluged** (catastrophe) with papers on the last day of the semester.

    註解　狂湧而至 (動詞，被動式；同義字爲名詞)

208. A serious **onslaught** (assault) against poverty is what is needed if the masses of poor are to be helped.

    註解　猛攻 (名詞)

209. When people in the small town needed advice, they always sought out Mr. Peter, who was regarded as sort of a(n) **oracle** (prophet) by his friends.

    註解　預言者，先知 (名詞)

210. Suzy **contrived** (concocted) an excuse to leave the house last night by saying that she absolutely had to borrow John's book.

    註解　設法，編設 (動詞)

211. The invading force coldly **spurned** (scorned) all offers of surrender and utterly destroyed the defending garrison to the last man.

    註解　擯斥，踢開 (動詞)

212. It was no accident that the astronauts aboard Apollo II were a **congenial** (suitable) group; the success of the entire mission rested on their ability to function flawlessly as a team.

    註解　適合的，意氣相投的 (形容詞)

213. Bill's adviser was most unsympathetic about his fear of numbers and insisted that his program be **comprised** (composed) of equal parts of arts and science.

    註解　包括，構成 (動詞，被動式)

214. The courses John elected to take **constituted** (formed) a very narrow, one sided program of studies.

   > 註解 構造 (動詞)

215. It takes a great deal of courage for a performer to face the taunts and **derision** (mock) of a hostile audience.

   > 註解 嘲笑，愚弄 (名詞)

216. The teacher refused to be **jeered** (taunted) by students hecklers and left the Washington campus in a huff.

   > 註解 嘲弄 (不定詞，被動式)

217. The forest ranger is the **sole** (solitary) inhabitant of this section of wilderness.

   > 註解 唯一的，孤獨的 (形容詞)

218. Mark's **audacious** (imprudent) behavior lately is quite a contrast to his mild manner as a small boy.

   > 註解 無禮的，輕率的 (形容詞)

219. Because Joe's health is not up to **par** (parity), the doctor wants to run a series of tests to determine the reason.

   > 註解 標準，常態，同等 (名詞)

220. After a long argument Michael finally **conceded** (yielded) one small point to Harry, and this act led to an ultimate resolution.

   > 註解 承認，退讓 (動詞)

221. In view of the technical difficulties aboard the service module, the only **conceivable** (devisable) course of action was to abort the mission and attempt to bring the Apollo 13 spacecraft back to earth as soon as possible.

   > 註解 可料到的 (形容詞)

222. Sydney Carton, secure in the nobleness of his intention, was able to maintain his **composure** (tranquility) even as he approached the guillotine.

   > 註解 沉著，鎮靜 (名詞)

223. Many people were convinced that the murder of eight nurse in 1966 could have only been the work of a **maniac** (insanity).

   > 註解 瘋子，瘋狂 (名詞)

224. After winning the beauty contest, Linda was almost crushed by a **throng** (swarm) of friends wanting to congratulate her.

   > 註解 眾多，群 (名詞)

225. The senator's **decisive** (fateful) answer to the question put an end to the speculation as to his position on the issue.

   註解 堅定的，致命的 (形容詞)

226. The failure of the Chess Club was probably the result of the **friction** (attrition) between officers who found it impossible to work together.

   註解 衝突，磨損 (名詞)

227. Billy **pelted** (peppered) the passing car with gravel from the drive.

   註解 投擲，密擊 (動詞)

228. The **episode** (incident) of his being caught stealing watermelons from Farmer Brown's patch is one Father never told us until we were adults.

   註解 插曲，事件 (名詞)

229. The band of rebels **routed** (subjugated) the colonial force by utilizing surprise tactics and sabotage.

   註解 安排，征服 (動詞)

230. A number of delegates threatened to **sever** (sunder) all connections with the party and to support none of the candidates.

   註解 切斷，斷絕 (不定詞)

231. By **splicing** (joining) the two ropes together we had enough line to hang a swing from a high limb in the apple tree.

   註解 接合 (動名詞)

232. The cruel jockey beat his horse with **fervor** (ardor) in order to make him run faster.

   註解 熱心 (名詞)

233. Last summer, discontent in the ghetto areas of the cities began to **ferment** (agitate) until city officials feared the outbreak of violence.

   註解 紛擾，鼓動 (不定詞)

234. Harold's **anguish** (torment) from his extensive burns could not be completely dulled by drugs.

   註解 痛苦，煩惱 (名詞)

235. Mr. Roberts was appointed to **dole** (ration) out the clothing to the flood victims.

   註解 少量捐，布施 (不定詞)

236. The two teams fought a **grueling** (exhausting) battle on the muddy football field.

     註解 筋疲力盡的，耗盡的 (形容詞)

237. John's **ostentation** (pompousness) in driving his flashy new car slowly around and around the block in his old neighborhood was noted by Judy and her friends.

     註解 誇張，自大 (名詞)

238. Jack's **ostensible** (conspicuous) reason for leaving class was to get a book; but in reality, he wanted to visit with Bill who was waiting in the hall.

     註解 假裝的，顯著的 (形容詞)

239. All of Susan's carefully made plans came to **naught** (nonexistence) because of her unexpected illness.

     註解 零，不存在 (名詞)

240. Houdini performed **stupendous** (awesome) feats of magic that left the audience amazed.

     註解 驚人的，令人敬畏的 (形容詞)

241. The **sanctity** (sacredness) of the ancient temple was violated by the tourists who did not realize they were forbidden to enter.

     註解 神聖，宗教上 (名詞)

242. Behavior **sanctioned** (authorized) as desirable by one society may be condemned by another, causing friction when the two groups intermingle.

     註解 認可，制裁 (過去分詞)

243. Mayor Welmon's speech was so **pompous** (pretentious) and full of self-importance that it disgusted most of his audience.

     註解 自大的，自負的 (形容詞)

244. Eloise made a mistake on the sales slip she was writing so she had to **void** (empty) it and start over again.

     註解 作廢，註銷 (不定詞)

245. A good news **commentary** (critique) reports all sides of a story fairly.

     註解 評語，批評 (動詞)

246. In his **skirmish** (scuffle) with the neighbor's dog, your cat seems to have received no injuries.

     註解 小爭論 (名詞)

247. The attorney for the defense was such a skillful orator that he nearly had the entire courtroom in tears, on behalf of his client, he **beseeched** (entreated) the judge not to impose the death penalty.

    註解　哀求 (動詞)

248. Peter **slavishly** (obsequiously) followed every whim of his wealthy uncle in hopes of being included in his will.

    註解　卑屈地，無獨立地 (副詞)

249. The Women's Liberation Movement works for the **emancipation** (liberation) of the female from what they consider to be a secondary role in society.

    註解　解放，獲得自由 (名詞)

250. The law classifies defamation of character as **libel** (slander) if it is printed and slander if it is oral.

    註解　文字誹謗，造謠 (名詞)

251. The **bleak** (dreary) appearance of the little room in the rundown hotel added to the young man's feeling if hopelessness.

    註解　淒涼的 (形容詞)

252. I expected the **outlay** (expenditure) for office furnishings to be much greater than it was.

    註解　費用，開支 (名詞)

253. Tim **relishes** (appreciates) the homemade bread baked by his grandmother, whom he visits in Oklahoma every summer.

    註解　品嚐，賞識 (動詞)

254. Difficulty in the middle ear generally results in a loss of **equilibrium** (balance), causing one to be dizzy and unable to walk in a straight line.

    註解　平衡 (名詞)

255. Michael **retorted** (rejoindered) in the same tone used by the boys who jeered and taunted him.

    註解　反擊，反駁 (動詞)

256. The Allied command post was situated in a bombproof bunker buried deep in the earth beneath ten cubic yards of concrete **reinforced** (fortify) with steel.

    註解　增強 (動詞)

257. David never developed into a first-rate pool player because he couldn't **banish** (subdue) his tendency to crumble under pressure.

    註解 忘卻，克服 (動詞)

258. The souring of milk is **retarded** (obstructed) by refrigeration.

    註解 延緩，阻隔 (動詞，被動式)

259. In an effort to enforce a **curb** (repression) on company spending, the president took away the executives' unlimited accounts.

    註解 抑制 (名詞)

260. When given a choice of solutions Cynthia is **prone** (bent) to take the easiest one available.

    註解 傾向的 (形容詞)

261. Although Tim considers himself to be **burly** (husky), I think he's just fat.

    註解 壯碩的 (形容詞)

262. Two small mice **scuttled** (scurried) back and forth under our cots that first night at camp.

    註解 倉皇的 (形容詞)

263. Because Mr. Mitchell is **prodigal** (extravagant), he has brought himself to bankruptcy.

    註解 揮霍的，浪費的 (形容詞)

264. Peggy's **aspiration** (desire) to be a school teacher is soon to be realized because she has been hired for a position in Martin's elementary school.

    註解 渴望 (名詞)

265. The sky darkened and the wind howled **forebodingly** (pretendingly) prior to the onset of the destructive storm.

    註解 預兆地，主張地 (副詞)

266. To **propagate** (multiply) the idea of hiring teen-agers during the summer, a group of civic leaders contacted every employer in the city.

    註解 宣傳，增多 (不定詞)

267. The newspaper reported that the sergeant was decorated for his **prowess** (valor) in battle.

    註解 英勇 (名詞)

268. The **troubadour** (minstrel) went from town to town amusing the idlers in the taverns with his songs of love and valor.

    註解 吟遊詩人 (名詞，Troubador 原爲義大利詩人)

269. The three drops of strong dye quickly **diffused** (scattered) in the water, turning the sea around the life raft a brilliant orange.
     註解 擴散 (動詞)

270. I never saw a man do such a **prodigious** (stupendous) amount of work for so little reward as Mr. Chen does is his garden.
     註解 龐大的，驚人的 (形容詞)

271. Charles Dickens portrays Bill Sykes as a **rogue** (scoundrel), evil beyond all description.
     註解 流氓，無賴 (名詞)

272. Our chemistry class watched the slow **disintegration** (dissolution) of a sugar cube in a glass of water while the teacher explained the differences between solutions and suspensions.
     註解 分解，溶解 (名詞)

273. It is difficult for an American to **procure** (secure) a work permit in France.
     註解 取得 (不定詞)

274. Throughout history the peasant has tended to blame the wealthy **aristocracy** (nobility) for his trouble.
     註解 貴族，上流社會 (名詞)

275. I have laid a trap for the mole who is ruining my garden, but he seems too **wily** (crafty) to be caught by it.
     註解 狡詐的 (形容詞)

276. The thoughts of most people speaking extemporaneously are rarely meaningful or **profound** (intense).
     註解 深刻的，強烈的 (形容詞)

277. A democratic leader **delegates** (disseminates) authority and responsibility to others.
     註解 委派，散布 (動詞)

278. The campus library was able to build a new wing because it had a rich **benefactor** (patron).
     註解 施主，贊助人 (名詞)

279. The elegant decorations **transformed** (changed) the gym into a starlit ballroom.
     註解 改變 (動詞)

280. His **fidelity** (dedication) to the ill-fated project was commendable.

> 註解　節操，奉獻 (名詞)

281. The captor told the hostages to assume a **prone** (face-down) position on the floor.

> 註解　傾向，面向 (名詞)

282. Peter was an **agile** (active) and athletic.

> 註解　敏捷的 (形容詞)

283. The **uproarious** (clamorous) reaction to the proposed convinced the union leaders to abandon it.

> 註解　騷動的，吵鬧的 (形容詞)

284. A hush fell over the guests who had **gathered** (assembled) for the wedding celebration.

> 註解　集合 (動詞，完成式)

285. Volunteer firefighters valiantly tried to extinguish the **raging** (intense) forest fire.

> 註解　蔓延的，劇烈的 (形容詞)

286. When it comes to buying clothes, Herman is **impetuous** (impulsive).

> 註解　衝動的 (形容詞)

287. Mathematics is a **compulsory** (required) subject in American high school.

> 註解　必修的，強迫的 (形容詞)

288. The **splendor** (magnificence) of the spring morning was breathtaking.

> 註解　光彩，華麗 (名詞)

289. Many millionaires become **eccentric** (peculiar) in their old age.

> 註解　古怪的 (形容詞)

290. After discussing the matter with the bank manager, John **instantly** (immediately) received his loan.

> 註解　立刻地 (副詞)

291. He made an obscene **gesture** (motion) before leaving the counselor's office.

> 註解　手勢，動作 (名詞)

292. The nurse was dismissed because she was found to be **negligent** (remiss).

> 註解　疏忽的 (形容詞)

293. The **proprietor** (owner) of the inn was a corpulent man.

> 註解　業主，所有人 (名詞)

294. The snow was so heavy that it **obliterated** (effaced) the highway.

    註解 消除 (動詞)

295. The fugitive **eluded** (evaded) capture for more than ten years.

    註解 逃脫 (動詞)

296. That new soap made her face **taut** (tight).

    註解 整潔的 (形容詞)

297. The policeman's **alert** (vigilant) mind caught the suspect's lies.

    註解 警覺的 (形容詞)

298. As we approached the pyramids, a **massive** (immense) stone sphinx greeted us at the entrance.

    註解 重大的 (形容詞)

299. The teacher picked up the student's book and **scrutinized** (examined) it.

    註解 細查 (動詞)

300. The interviewer promised not to **divulge** (reveal) the source of his information.

    註解 洩露 (不定詞)

301. The warranty guaranteed that all **defective** (imperfect) parts would be replaced without charge.

    註解 有缺點的 (形容詞)

302. It was difficult to find the missing papers on Gary's **cluttered** (littered) desk.

    註解 雜亂的 (形容詞)

303. During the Inquisition, heretics **tortured** (persecuted) for their religious beliefs.

    註解 拷問，迫害 (動詞)

304. Imagine the advertiser's **humiliation** (chagrin) when he realized that he had put the wrong date in the ad.

    註解 丟臉，懊惱 (名詞)

305. Every effort was made to reduce the budget **greatly** (substantially).

    註解 實際地，大致地 (副詞)

306. **Recurrent** (Intermittent) showers were forecast for the day.

    註解 間歇的，周期性的 (形容詞)

307. The plant manager was promoted to an **administrative** (executive) position.

　　註解　行政上的，執行的 (形容詞)

308. John felt **sure** (confident) about his grade on the test he had just taken.

　　註解　自信的 (形容詞)

309. The once beautiful flowers in the vase had **withered** (wilted).

　　註解　枯萎的 (形容詞)

310. Ponce de Le'on believed that the waters of the Fountain of Youth had the power to **rejuvenate** (make one young).

　　註解　恢復活力 (不定詞)

311. The gymnast's exercise made her feel **stimulated** (exhilarated).

　　註解　激勵的 (形容詞)

312. There is a campaign against those hunters who mercilessly **slaughter** (kill) baby seals.

　　註解　屠殺 (動詞)

313. Striding **quickly** (briskly) down the cobblestone road, she caught her shoe between the bricks.

　　註解　敏捷地 (副詞)

314. The speaker walked **assuredly** (confidently) and quickly to the podium.

　　註解　確信地 (副詞)

315. That matter was totally **alien** (irrelevant) to the discussion at hand.

　　註解　不相關的，相反的 (形容詞)

316. The new teacher was appalled at the **chaotic** (disorderly) condition of her classroom.

　　註解　混亂的 (形容詞)

317. The young man **winced** (flinched) in pain as the doctor stitched up the gash in his arm.

　　註解　退縮 (動詞)

318. Having fasted for five days, the woman was **famished** (starved).

　　註解　飢餓的 (形容詞)

319. The groom's hand **fondled** (caressed) the soft mane of the horse.

　　註解　撫弄 (動詞)

320. Beethoven, having composed symphonies at three, was considered **precocious** (gifted).

    > 註解 早熟的，天才的 (形容詞)

321. Despite the raging storm outside, the speaker did not **deviate** (depart) from his lecture.

    > 註解 離題，離開 (動詞)

322. The toxic material on the derailed train **contaminated** (polluted) the atmosphere.

    > 註解 污染 (動詞)

323. The gas company **detected** (discovered) a leak in the main line and evacuated all the tenants of the building.

    > 註解 發現 (動詞)

324. That the world is flat was an idea Columbas helped prove **fallacious** (deceptive).

    > 註解 謬誤的 (形容詞)

325. The condemned man ate very slowly in order to **savor** (relish) every bite of his last meal.

    > 註解 品嚐 (不定詞)

326. Because she is so **saucy** (insolent) with them, the clerk dread having Denise come into the store.

    > 註解 魯莽的 無禮的 (形容詞)

327. A poorly adjusted carburetor was the cause of the car's **inordinate** (extravagant) use of gasoline.

    > 註解 過度的，浪費的 (形容詞)

328. Frustrated by the poor exam grade, Bill **gnashed** (grinded) his teeth in anger.

    > 註解 磨(牙)，切(齒) (動詞)

329. Mr. Thompson is rather **cynical** (sarcastic) about the honesty of students since he has seen so much cheating.

    > 註解 冷嘲的，挖苦的 (形容詞)

330. The **supple** (limber) boughs of the willow tree bent with the wind but did not break.

    > 註解 柔軟的 (形容詞)

331. After the **partition** (distribution) of India into India and Pakistan, there was a long period of bloodshed.

    註解 分隔 (名詞)

332. Even the least interested students were **enthralled** (captivate) by Lady Macbeth's sleepwalking scene.

    註解 迷惑 (動詞，被動式)

333. An increase in wind **velocity** (tempo) often indicates the approach of storm.

    註解 速度 (名詞)

334. Although he has been gone many years, his face is deeply **etched** (engraved) in my memory.

    註解 深印 (動詞，被動式)

335. The condemned criminal remained in prison **pending** (imminent) a decision on an appeal which might prevent his execution.

    註解 未決定的，逼近的 (形容詞)

336. He is likely to exhibit a **vile** (repulsive) temper if he does not get his way.

    註解 惡劣的 (形容詞)

337. Jennifer constantly **fondled** (cuddled) the class ring which Harry gave her when he graduated.

    註解 撫弄 (動詞)

338. The **enactment** (decree) of a gun-control law would help to some extent in crime control.

    註解 法規，法令 (名詞)

339. The **tufts** (clumps) of wild onions gave the lawn a ragged appearance.

    註解 叢塊 (動詞)

340. As the bells **pealed** (resounded) from the little church, people could be seen hurrying to worship.

    註解 鐘聲，回聲 (動詞)

341. According to Article Seventeen of the Constitution, **suffrage** (franchise) cannot be denied citizens of the United States on account of race, color or previous conditions of servitude.

    註解 投票權，經銷權 (名詞)

342. Because Lucy spent money lavishly, she soon **incurred** (contracted) many debts.

   註解　遭遇 (動詞)

343. Because Sarah never helped with the dishes, she **competent** (adequate) the anger of her overworked mother.

   註解　能幹的，適當的 (形容詞)

344. Being an obedient child, Laurie did not **demur** (vacillate) when her mother called her in from playing hide-and-seek.

   註解　抗議，猶疑不決 (動詞)

345. The **demure** (prim) little old lady scarcely raised her eyes from her plate as she sat eating her lunch in the bus station restaurant.

   註解　嚴肅的，端端正正的 (形容詞)

346. The lightning caused a **cleft** (aperture) in the giant oak tree that will surely cause it to die.

   註解　裂縫，孔隙 (名詞)

347. Since the flood, the woods are so **infested** (overruned) with poisonous snakes that it is dangerous to walk through them.

   註解　蔓生的，群居的 (形容詞)

348. Lucy's occasional, half-hearted help with the dishes did not **compensate** (reimburse) for all the work she caused me by being so messy.

   註解　賠償 (動詞)

349. America has always been considered a **stronghold** (fortress) of freedom and democracy by the European countries.

   註解　堡壘 (名詞)

350. In the **distraction** (frenzy) of preparation for the meeting, I mislaid my lecture notes which I had so carefully prepared.

   註解　恐慌，心煩 (名詞)

351. A **hubbub** (flurry) of excitement preceded the entrance of the beam, but the crowd soon settled themselves to watch the tense game.

   註解　嘈雜，擾亂 (名詞)

352. Mary slipped like a cat through the crowd, trying not to **jostle** (elbow) anyone.

   註解　推擠 (不定詞)

353. The chemistry instructor explained that the forces of **cohesion** (adhesion) between atoms make it very difficult to separate a water molecule into its two atoms of hydrogen and one of oxygen.

    | 註解 | 凝結，附著 (名詞)

354. Many youth are disgusted by the **hypocrisy** (pretense) they see in some adults, who preach one kind of behavior while they practice quite the opposite.

    | 註解 | 偽善，虛偽 (名詞)

355. Sally's birthday **coincides** (conjugates) with the birthday of our country; both are on the Fourth of July.

    | 註解 | 符合，一致 (動詞)

356. Whenever my bulldog is well fed, he becomes quite **amiable** (affable) and allows almost anyone to pat his head.

    | 註解 | 友善的 (形容詞)

357. Henry's bitter words indicate that his **animosity** (malice) toward his cousin has not lessened over the years.

    | 註解 | 仇恨 (名詞)

358. The season Ruth is elected to so many positions of prestige is that people know she will never **evade** (shirk) the duties involved.

    | 註解 | 逃避 (動詞)

359. Because of his interest and understanding of youth, Mr. Green has always had considerable **weight** (prestige) among the teen-age group.

    | 註解 | 聲望，分量 (名詞)

360. James **allegedly** (assertablly) left the scene of the accident before the highway patrol arrived, but he continues to deny it.

    | 註解 | 宣稱地，辯護地 (副詞)

361. Elizabeth excused herself from the yearbook meeting on the **fabrication** (pretense) of a doctor's appointment in town, when in reality she wanted to go shopping for a new sweater.

    | 註解 | 捏造 (名詞)

362. Susan, a vain little girl is especially **impressionable** (susceptible) to flattery.

    | 註解 | 易受感動的 (形容詞)

363. **Turmoil** (bedlam) erupted in the classroom as a mangy terrier wandered in the door, sniffed inquisitively at the teacher's ankles, and then dashed down the center aisle with four students in mad pursuit.

    註解　騷動 (名詞)

364. Do not **perplex** (confound) the committee more by bringing up additional problems; it is already completely confused by the issues that are under discussion.

    註解　混淆，迷惑 (動詞)

365. I think you will enjoy fishing up at our lake; the accommodation are **rustic** (rough) but comfortable.

    註解　質樸的 (形容詞)

366. Some teachers feel that there is no place for **glee** (mirth) in the classroom; others do not object to a light atmosphere.

    註解　歡樂 (名詞)

367. My father, after losing $20 to a pickpocket at the bus station, could do nothing but **bemoan** (lament).

    註解　惋惜，悲傷 (動詞)

368. When Martha was stopped on her way home from school, she acted **judiciously** (prudently) in refusing the ride from the strange man.

    註解　謹慎地 (副詞)

369. There is nothing more **insolent** (brazen) than a parakeet who thinks she can flirt with a cat without getting hurt.

    註解　無禮的，面如黃銅的 (形容詞)

370. In our society it is **conventional** (customary), thought not particularly fair, for the young man to pay the entire cost of a date.

    註解　傳統的 (形容詞)

371. To many in our society money is the only **deity** (God).

    註解　神 (名詞)

372. My uncle Harold is a **devout** (pious) man who has based his entire life on the religious precepts of Christianity.

    註解　虔誠的 (形容詞)

373. Sandy has an old **idiosyncrasy** (quirk) of cleaning her fingernails before she comes indoors.

    註解　癖性 (名詞)

374. A man with a wide **latitude** (scope) of interests and understanding is needed to work with students who come to this school from all over the country.

　　　註解　思維，眼界 (名詞)

375. A doctor who devotes his life to treating the natives in some underdeveloped county is probably doing it for humanitarian reasons rather than **avaricious** (mercenary) ones, since the pay involved is likely to be quite small.

　　　註解　貪財的，爲錢而工作的 (形容詞)

376. Although many people are familiar with extra-sensory perception, relatively few efforts have been made to investigate this **phenomenon** (marvel) in a scientific fashion.

　　　註解　現象 (名詞)

377. Make sure you read the fine print before you give **assent** (acceding) by signing your name to the contract.

　　　註解　同意，讓步 (名詞)

378. A treaty to **ban** (taboo) the testing of nuclear weapons has been adamantly refused by Red China.

　　　註解　禁止 (不定詞)

379. You need not be **loath** (reluctant) to admit a mistake, because anyone can make one.

　　　註解　不願意的 (形容詞)

380. Because Bill **loathes** (abominates) injustice, he campaigned fervently for passage of the open-housing bill.

　　　註解　厭惡 (動詞)

381. I would consider Uncle Harry a **connoisseur** (expert) of restaurants in the city where he has lived for twenty years.

　　　註解　行家 (名詞)

382. It will be impossible to cultivate those **saturated** (sodden) fields for a long time even though the rain has ceased.

　　　註解　浸透 (動詞)

383. My **client** (patronage) of the Martin Bank began when I moved here thirty-four years ago, and I have been a steady customer ever since.

　　　註解　顧客 (名詞)

384. The network stopped its continuous coverage of the space flight after the lift-off but promised to interrupt its programming with any **subsequent** (following) events of interest.

   註解　接續的 (形容詞)

385. The rioting convicts were **subdued** (subjugated) (overcame) by the use of tear gas.

   註解　壓制 (動詞，被動式)

386. In recent years the people of Greece have been **burdened** (suppressed) by a harsh totalitarian government.

   註解　鎮壓 (動詞，完成被動式)

387. This new rule **supplants** (supersedes) all eight rules listed on page twenty of the manual.

   註解　取代 (動詞)

388. Martha **accentuated** (emphasized) the blueness of her eyes by the artful use of eye shadow.

   註解　強調 (動詞)

389. The **dominion** (sovereignty) of the king was unquestioned by his subjects even though they objected to his tyranny.

   註解　統治權 (名詞)

390. The sub-freezing temperature had caused a **crystalline** (translucent) covering of ice to form on the window.

   註解　透明的 (形容詞)

391. There's no need to be so **clandestine** (furtive) about your actions, for I know what you are trying to do.

   註解　偷偷的 (形容詞)

392. Jane answered the woman's prying questions **curtly** (brusquely), but I could hardly blame her for her ungracious manner under the circumstances.

   註解　粗率地 (副詞)

393. Keith and Mark were startled to discover that their **secluded** (cloistered) fishing hole was being used by other fishermen.

   註解　隔離的 (形容詞)

394. The crowd gathered quietly and humbly to **venerate** (revere) the great bishop.

　　註解　崇拜 (不定詞)

395. Because Molly was **apprehensive** (alarmed) about her approaching plane trip, I suggested that she cancel her reservations and go by train.

　　註解　憂慮的 (形容詞)

396. The old pine tree leaned **obliquely** (tiltedly), evidently as a result of the strong north winds.

　　註解　歪斜地 (副詞)

397. Spotting an obvious error in his new dictionary, Jim came to the startling realization that even the experts are **fallible** (debatable).

　　註解　易犯錯的 (形容詞)

398. When the folk singers began the first notes of "Where Have All the Flowers Gone?" there was a **spontaneous** (impromptu) reaction on the part of the crowd to begin singing along.

　　註解　自發的 (形容詞)

399. Keeping a perfectly neat house was such a(n) **obsession** (mania) with Hazel that she made us remove our shoes before entering the living room.

　　註解　身心困擾 (名詞)

400. Someone should report that man to the **humane** (benevolent) society for beating his dog.

　　註解　慈善的 (形容詞)

401. All clues had been **obliterated** (annihilated) by the rain, leaving the detective no sign of which direction the burglar.

　　註解　消滅 (動詞，完成被動式)

402. Mr. Wels hid his evil practices under a **veneer** (façade) of respectability.

　　註解　外表 (名詞)

403. Mr. Chip went back to his old home town to **flaunt** (flourish) his new wealth before his old neighbors.

　　註解　炫耀，裝飾 (不定詞)

404. The tired boy lays his full length, **prostrates** (inclines) on the floor in front of he fireplace.

　　註解　倒臥 (動詞)

405. Tom paddled his canoe dangerously near the **brink** (verge) of the waterfall.

   註解　邊緣 (名詞)

406. The **seizure** (confiscation) of the burglar's cache of stolen goods was effected by the police without a hitch.

   註解　奪取物，沒收 (名詞)

407. Theodore is a sullen boy who answers his teachers' questions with a **terse** (blunt) monosyllable.

   註解　簡明的 (形容詞)

408. To enter the monastery you must **forsake** (repudiate) the pleasures of the flesh and dedicate yourself to the Lord.

   註解　放棄 (動詞)

409. The only **legacy** (heritage) Mr. White left was the memory of his life spent in service for others.

   註解　遺書 (名詞)

410. My father **commutes** (interchanges) from our home to work in Chicago every day.

   註解　變換 (動詞)

411. Noting that her son's blue jeans were uncomfortably tight, the mother commented on their **snug** (cozy) fit.

   註解　舒適的 (形容詞，同 cosy)

412. A patriotic man does not **falter** (totter) in striving for those goals that are in his country's best interests.

   註解　蹣跚，搖動 (動詞)

413. With the **throttle** (accelerator) wide open, the midget racer roared into the lead.

   註解　加速器 (名詞)

414. Root beer usually has a delicious **froth** (foam) on top which is why many people drink it.

   註解　泡沫 (名詞)

415. Merchandise that has **flaws** (fissure) is sometimes labeled "imperfect" and sold at a reduced price.

   註解　瑕疵，裂縫 (名詞)

416. The object of the police search was to **apprehend** (capture) the suspect so that he could be questioned about the crime.

> 註解　捕捉 (不定詞)

417. "This part is not turning; the rust keeps it from **pivot** (axis) on its shaft."

> 註解　中心點，軸

418. Some **dialects** (idioms) of Pennsylvania are the result of speech patterns of the Dutch and Germans who settled there.

> 註解　方言 (名詞)

419. The teacher explained that several ancient peoples communicated through the use of **cuneiform** (wedge-shaped writing), an unusual form of writing involving a series of wedge-shaped marks.

> 註解　楔形文字 (名詞)

420. From his neatly combed hair and spotlessly clean clothes, it was easy to see that Robert was **impeccable** (perfect) in his personal habits.

> 註解　無瑕疵的 (形容詞)

421. If a missile carrying a nuclear warhead hit San Francisco, all buildings within five miles of "ground zero" would be **razed** (destroyed).

> 註解　消逝的 (動詞，被動式)

422. Lee was eager to express his **condolence** (sympathy) to Jerry after his father was in a serious accident.

> 註解　哀悼 (名詞)

423. I think it is **futile** (useless) for you to try to earn an A this semester; presently you have D-average and only one week remains in the term.

> 註解　徒勞的 (形容詞)

424. The present **economic** (business) conditions have discouraged many investors from putting more money into the stock market.

> 註解　經濟的 (形容詞)

425. Since their small apartment could not accommodate their vast collection of antique furniture, Evelyn and Ted moved into a more **commodious** (roomy) one.

> 註解　寬敞的 (形容詞)

426. An **intricate** (complex) design is pretty and eye-catching; on the other hand, a simple one would be easier to produce.

> 註解　複雜的 (形容詞)

427. Charlie's biggest fault is that he **procrastinates** (puts things off); that is, he never does today what he can put off until tomorrow.

   註解　拖延 (動詞)

428. The ancient Romans are considered by most people to have been quite **bellicose** (warlike) because of their frequent battles.

   註解　好爭吵的 (形容詞)

429. A **dynamic** (energetic) speaker is more likely to hold the interest of his audience than a weak and sluggish one.

   註解　精力充沛的 (形容詞)

430. Unable to **devise** (scheme) a plan of escape, the prisoner reluctantly let his dreams of freedom become memories.

   註解　計劃 (不定詞)

431. We knew what we were in store for the night Mother brought home an automatic food chopper. Before the novelty wore off, we were served every kind of **shredded** (ripped) vegetable imaginable.

   註解　切碎的 (形容詞)

432. The wealthy debutante **dabbled** (splashed) in antique but did not really take it seriously.

   註解　涉獵 (動詞)

433. When the rescuers found the boys who had been lost, they were **quaking** (trembling) from cold and exposure.

   註解　發抖 (動詞，進行式)

434. The director of a play must **manipulate** (maneuver) the cast to achieve the type of production he desires.

   註解　操縱 (動詞)

435. The **barbarism** (savagism) of the Germanic tribes appalled the Romans, who considered Roman civilization superior to any others.

   註解　野蠻 (名詞)

436. The refugee from East Germany found a **haven** (sanctuary) in the tree world.

   註解　庇護所 (名詞)

437. The outlaws **ruthlessly** (cruelly) took over the small town, stealing from the businessmen and murdering those who interfered.

   註解　無情地 (副詞)

438. As the plane took off and began to **ascend** (soar), the fire from the right engine warned us that something was wrong.

   | 註解 | 上升 (不定詞)

439. "Marsha's **sarcasm** (ridicule) has offended me many times, and I feel that her bitter remarks are out of place" said Sally.

   | 註解 | 譏笑 (名詞)

440. Diplomatic **immunity** (exemption) protects official representatives of foreign countries from arrest while serving in the United States.

   | 註解 | 免除 (名詞)

441. "**Recline** (Repose) on the couch and perhaps your headache will go away", advised the school nurse.

   | 註解 | 橫臥 (動詞)

442. Television networks may **censor** (evaluate) program that contain material unsuitable for general viewing, thus preventing parts of the show from appearing on the air.

   | 註解 | 檢查 (動詞)

443. In recent years the United States Senate has rarely formally **censured** (rebuked) on of its members for some wrongdoing.

   | 註解 | 責難 (動詞，完成式)

444. Clothes made with some of the newly-developed synthetic fibers are so **durable** (enduring) they look practically new after years of wear.

   | 註解 | 耐久的 (形容詞)

445. The students expressed their **accord** (harmony) on one point: no one wanted the homework load increased.

   | 註解 | 協調，一致 (名詞)

446. The maid caught her hand in the wringer of the washing machine and **mangled** (mutilated) it badly.

   | 註解 | 切斷 (動詞)

447. **Anxiety** (Foreboding) is a common complaint today caused by the tension of our hectic way of living.

   | 註解 | 不安，預感 (名詞)

448. Following the trial, the fifteen-year-old burglar was kept in the **custody** (detention) of the court rather than being sent home.

   | 註解 | 監視，拘禁 (名詞)

449. An investigation following the collapse of the bridge showed that the contractor had skimped (**scrimped**) on the materials used and that this had weakened the structure.

   註解 供給不足，縮減 (動詞，完成式)

450. The **glint** (sparkle) of light in the darkness of the room indicated where the window had been boarded over.

   註解 閃光 (名詞)

451. Although my great grandfather's **livelihood** (living) was from blacksmithing, I could not earn a living at that today.

   註解 生計 (名詞)

452. The enemy was so ruthless in the conduct of the war they would not consent to a **truce** (cease-fire) for the religious holidays.

   註解 停戰 (名詞)

453. Because Aunt Myra has had a **lapse** (interruption) of memory, she has no recollection of her accident.

   註解 差錯，中斷 (名詞)

454. "I enjoy spy movies because I find **intrigue** (conspiracy) exciting", whispered Marcie to her mother as they watched the film.

   註解 陰謀 (名詞)

455. The experiment must be carried out **precisely** (explicitly) so that every step is correct, or the results will not be valid.

   註解 正確地 (副詞)

456. Since the threatening note was **anonymous** (unknown), the police were baffled as to who sent it.

   註解 匿名的 (形容詞)

457. The **unanimous** (agreeing) decision of the club members was to plan the trip for June since that date was convenient for everyone.

   註解 全體一致的 (形容詞)

458. The **supplement** (reinforcement) sent along with book included graphs that explained the research.

   註解 補充，增援 (名詞)

459. The **miscellany** (diversity) of items brought to the rummage sale covered everything imaginable.

   註解 混合 (名詞)

460. Since the **glen** (cove) was not visible from the road, the secluded valley was not overrun with tourists.

　　註解　小彎 (名詞)

461. The children were badly mauled by the grizzly bear when they accidently stumbled upon him leaving his **lair** (den).

　　註解　藏身地，獸穴 (名詞)

462. Everyone's appetite increased as the succulent **aroma** (fragrance) of the Thanksgiving turkey spread throughout the house.

　　註解　香味 (名詞)

463. As the river rose near to flood stage, the mayor issued an order to **fortify** (bolster) the dam.

　　註解　加強，支撐 (不定詞)

464. While separated from his family, the young child felt lost and **forlorn** (woebegone).

　　註解　絕望的，憂愁的 (形容詞)

465. The president said that all club members should **participate** (partake) in the fund drive since it was a club project.

　　註解　參與，分享 (動詞)

466. United States foreign relations are conducted through elaborate **diplomatic** (suave) arrangements with other countries.

　　註解　圓滑的，溫和的 (形容詞)

467. The **penitent** (repentant) child climbed on his mother's lap and said he was sorry.

　　註解　後悔的 (形容詞)

468. The final **segment** (portion) of the musical has a rousing marching band routine.

　　註解　片斷 (名詞)

469. Since several of us had to leave the meeting early, we decided to **dispense** (allot) with the reading of the minutes and go directly to the treasurer's report.

　　註解　分配 (不定詞)

470. The attorney's **eloquent** (polished) defense of the defendant caused the jury to bring in a verdict of not guilty.

　　註解　潤飾的 (形容詞)

471. The dull games and boring lessons served to **stifle** (aid) the bright child's curiosity and interest.

   註解　抑止，促成 (不定詞)

472. There are two branches of study in chemistry: **organic** (living) chemistry and inorganic chemistry.

   註解　有機的，器官的 (形容詞)

473. Although I've never been there, the **allure** (enchantment) of Hawaii makes me want to live there someday.

   註解　誘惑 (名詞)

474. The watchdog guarded the grounds of the home as if it were his own personal **domain** (sphere).

   註解　領土 (名詞)

475. Many people believe the **illusion** (fantasy) that great wealth brings great happiness.

   註解　幻想 (名詞)

476. The purpose of the audit is to **ascertain** (discover) the total amount of money now held by the company.

   註解　發現 (不定詞)

477. The high winds had overturned the trash cans and had **strewn** (broadcasted) trash all over the yard.

   註解　散布 (動詞，完成式)

478. John was **brooding** (pondering) over the death of his dog when his mother found him on the porch and tried to cheer him up.

   註解　沉思 (動詞，進行式)

479. Due to a(n) **abrupt** (brusque) change in the schedule, no one was prepared for the assembly at 1:00 p.m.

   註解　突然的 (形容詞)

480. The hunters skinned the **carcass** (skeleton) of the deer.

   註解　動物的屍體 (名詞)

481. The cat **lurked** (skulked) in the corner of the room, waiting for the mouse to come out of his hole.

   註解　躲藏 (動詞)

482. A **colossal** (minute) oil refinery, covering over 100 acres and having over 200 building, is being planned for southern Louisiana.

> 註解　巨大的，大量的 (形容詞)

483. The scavengers picked up the **salvage** (rescue) from the wrecked ship as it drifted in toward shore.

> 註解　海難救助 (名詞)

484. Part of our national **heritage** (inheritance) is the historic homes of men like Jefferson and Lee.

> 註解　遺產 (名詞)

485. Although no flame was visible, the coals **smoldered** (smoked) for several hours under the grating of the fireplace.

> 註解　悶燒冒煙 (動詞)

486. Having no **offspring** (descendant) of his own, the old man treated his nephew as a son.

> 註解　後代 (名詞)

487. I have tried to **detach** (sever) myself from the situation and to be more objective, but I have not succeeded.

> 註解　分離 (不定詞)

488. When the ranchers caught the horse thief, they **lynched** (hanged) him without a trial.

> 註解　處死 (動詞)

489. After every member had signed the **pact** (alliance), the boys swore secrecy and loyalty toward their club.

> 註解　協定 (名詞)

490. The man was so **disfigured** (marred) by the accident that he was hardly recognizable to even his closest friends.

> 註解　損壞的 (形容詞)

491. Mother is so **sentimental** (feeling) that she always cries at weddings.

> 註解　感傷的 (形容詞)

492. Any additional comments would be **superfluous** (redundant) since Ellen has presented a thorough summary and nothing remains to be said.

> 註解　多餘的 (形容詞)

493. Because he **aspires** (yearns) to be a lawyer, Steven entered a pre-law program at college.

    註解 | 渴望 (動詞)

494. During World War 11, millions of European Jews were **annihilated** (butchered) under order from Hitler.

    註解 | 殘殺 (動詞，被動式)

495. When the gas tank exploded following the accident, the car was **consumed** (engrossed) be fire.

    註解 | 燒毀，壟斷 (動詞，被動式)

496. The young mother next door seems to **devote** (assign) every waking hour to caring for her new baby.

    註解 | 獻身 (不定詞)

497. The hungry children devoured the chocolate cake, even finishing the last **morsel** (tidbit) left on the platter.

    註解 | 少量、一小片 (名詞，同 titbit)

498. I **derived** (originated) my solution to the mystery by thinking about the suspects and their motives.

    註解 | 獲得，產生 (動詞)

499. The tiny kitten drenched by the rain looked so **pathetic** (pitiable) that I carried it into the house.

    註解 | 悲慘的 (形容詞)

500. While we finish **transacting** (enacting) the morning's business, you may wait in the outer office.

    註解 | 處理 (動名詞，finish 之後接 ing 不接 to)

501. The **profile** (silhouette) of the tree against the sky at sunset was so beautiful that the painter began to sketch the tree's outline.

    註解 | 輪廓，外形 (名詞)

502. As the **complexity** (intricacy) of her personal problems grew, Anne could not handle the involved difficulties herself, so she sought out a counselor.

    註解 | 複雜，難懂 (名詞)

503. The play's **climax** (apex) comes when the couple meet again after a ten-year separation and decide to marry.

    註解 | 最高潮 (名詞)

504. The magazine article **portrays** (depicts) the mayor's wife as a cold, ruthless woman who cares for no one but herself.

   註解 描畫 (動詞)

505. Unaware that he was **delinquent** (overdue) in paying his property taxes for the year, Dan was surprised to receive an overdue notice.

   註解 過期的 (形容詞)

506. The boisterous play of the children made it difficult for Aunt Belle to **meditate** (contemplate), so she asked the children to go outside.

   註解 沉思 (不定詞)

507. Since the contract requires that you make regular monthly payments, your failure to make these payments **terminates** (ends) the agreement.

   註解 終止 (動詞)

508. "I would love to be chosen the dancer in the play, but I know I don't have a chance," Madge said **wistfully** (longingly).

   註解 渴望地 (副詞)

509. The mayor decided to **survey** (scan) the community to determine if public opinion supported the proposed law.

   註解 審察 (不定詞)

510. "Shall I pretend to **swoon** (faint) if he proposes?" asked Sarah jokingly.

   註解 昏倒 (不定詞)

511. A student who is particularly **apt** (dexterous) in mathematics and likes to work with numbers should consider a career in the computer science field.

   註解 機巧的，擅長的 (形容詞)

512. When making an apple pie, you must **pare** (lessen) the apples to remove the skins.

   註解 剝開變小 (動詞)

513. "Quacks" are considered to be **fraud** (swindles) since they pretend to be licensed doctors and offer expensive cures and remedies that are useless to sick people.

   註解 欺騙，冒充 (名詞)

514. It is necessary to **dice** (mince) chicken finely to make chicken spread for sandwiches.

   註解 切碎 (不定詞)

515. The **potential** (capacity) for using atomic energy in industry is just being discovered; the future will reveal new and exciting uses for it.

    註解　可能性 (名詞)

516. Van Cliburn, the **illustrious** (eminent) young pianist, has toured many countries giving concerts.

    註解　著名的 (形容詞)

517. Weary from working long hours on the construction job, mark **plodded** (trudged).

    註解　疲累的走 (動詞)

518. The two children who had been missing for several hours were found **rambling** (sauntering) through the park, exploring anything that caught their interest.

    註解　閒逛 (動詞，進行式)

519. Although Alice tried to **alibi** (excuse) her way out of the serious accusation, her explanation was not accepted.

    註解　辯解 (不定詞)

520. Many people develop the habit of **squinting** (narrowing) even wen they are not in bright light.

    註解　狹窄 (名詞)

521. "Although a certain amount of **egotism** (boastfulness) is natural, a person should not be preoccupied with himself," explained the psychologist.

    註解　自負，自誇 (名詞)

522. The problem of finding a settlement agreeable to both sides in the war continues to **baffle** (puzzle) government leaders.

    註解　阻撓 (不定詞)

523. The decorator decided to **diversify** (modify) the color scheme in the house so that it would be more interesting.

    註解　變化，修飾 (不定詞)

524. The mayor ordered that crews be hired to **exterminate** (eradicate) the disease-carrying rate that were spreading an epidemic throughout the city.

    註解　消除 (不定詞)

525. Denied **access** (admittance) to the new hospital wing, the angry man sought another entrance.

    註解　進入 (名詞)

526. A few years ago, the **lyrics** (poetics) of many popular songs were almost meaningless; now they are often more important than the beat and melody.
    註解 歌詞 (名詞)

527. Since the farmer's death, the fields have been **bare** (arid) because there is no one to plow and plant them.
    註解 不毛之地的 (形容詞)

528. A porous object, like a sponge, is able to **retain** (preserve) water for a considerable amount of time.
    註解 保留 (不定詞)

529. Many factors **hindered** (clogged) completion of the civic center, but the most crucial delay was the apathy of a large numbers of citizens.
    註解 阻止 (動詞)

530. The **babble** (prattle) of the children at the birthday party was a pretty good indication that the young boys and girls were enjoying themselves.
    註解 閒談 (名詞)

531. The **ghastly** (hideous) vision of his dead uncle disturbed the scheming nephew for several months.
    註解 可怕的 (形容詞)

532. Although the dispatcher sympathized with the **plight** (predicament) of the woman who needed a taxi immediately, he explained that it would be at least half an hour before the cab arrived.
    註解 處境 (名詞)

533. Since most **proverbs** (adages) have stood the test of tie, there is generally much truth in these sayings.
    註解 格言 (名詞)

534. The **scanty** (meager) provisions barely lasted the climbers three days.
    註解 不足的 (形容詞)

535. Running for hours after his escape, the **fugitive** (escape) was exhausted and near death.
    註解 逃犯 (名詞)

536. Rubbing two sticks together is a primitive way to **ignite** (kindle) a fire.
    註解 點燃 (不定詞)

537. My English **tutor** (instructor), who has given me private lessons for three years, was born in Paris.

   註解　家教 (名詞)

538. The boy's **unique** (unequaled) batting stance may have looked ridiculous, but he was his team's best hitter.

   註解　獨特的 (形容詞)

539. The new store manager worked for a firm on the other side of town **prior** (previous) to coming her.

   註解　較早的 (形容詞)

540. Before taking out an insurance policy on her jewelry, Mother had an **appraisal** (assessment) made by a licensed jeweler.

   註解　估價 (名詞)

541. The **array** (attire) of military uniforms seen in the parade was dazzling to behold.

   註解　服裝 (名詞)

542. The unpredictable autumn winds caused the dead leaves to **swirl** (twist) across the yard in whirlwind fashion.

   註解　旋轉 (不定詞)

543. A cold shower in the morning makes your skin feel **tingly** (prickly) for hours.

   註解　刺痛的 (形容詞，feel 感官動詞接形容詞)

544. Several witnesses commented on the **sinister** (eerie) appearance of a tall man seen in the vicinity at the time of the fire.

   註解　邪惡的 (形容詞)

545. The strange visitors to her new boarder's room **perplexed** (mystified) the landlady, who could not imagine what they wanted.

   註解　困惑的 (形容詞)

546. The lion at the zoo may not look **ferocious** (fierce), but it can easily kill a man.

   註解　兇猛的 (形容詞，look 感官動詞接形容詞)

547. Although she is **arrogant** (haughty), she is also very bright, which is why so many people overlook her proud manner.

   註解　傲慢的 (形容詞)

548. Mr. Adams, suffering from **chronic** (habitual) heart disease, has not been able to participate in vigorous physical activity for several years.

   |註解| 慣性的 (形容詞)

549. A(n) **acute** (intense) attack of appendicitis, while serious, is usually not fatal today.

   |註解| 劇烈的 (形容詞)

550. Father's announcement **pertained** (related) to our family vacation, which he suggested be a trip to California.

   |註解| 關於 (動詞)

551. The guerilla fighters, **tactics** (strategies) were to surround the camp first, then capture the machine gun.

   |註解| 策略 (名詞)

552. "Even though I was **extravagant** (lavish) in buying this expensive dress, I hope to get much wear out of it", explained the young girl to her father.

   |註解| 浪費的 (形容詞)

553. The **peril** (hazard) of water and air pollution are not generally recognized for the serious threats they pose to our environment.

   |註解| 危險 (名詞)

554. The prosecuting attorney hoped the jury would **convict** (charge) the murderer and recommend the death penalty.

   |註解| 宣告有罪 (動詞)

555. "Since the grapefruit is **tart** (pungent), you might want to sprinkle it with sugar," suggested Grandmother.

   |註解| 酸的，辛辣的 (形容詞)

556. I **infer** (surmise) from his remarks that he thinks I am responsible for the accident.

   |註解| 推測 (動詞)

557. The magazine **implicated** (insinuated) that the mayor had engaged in deals with the crime syndicate even though it did not state so outright.

   |註解| 暗示 (動詞)

558. The **drab** (dull) appearance of the old farmhouse kitchen was considerably improved by a coat of paint.

   |註解| 單調的 (形容詞)

559. A good newspaper reporter always **verifies** (confirms) the facts of a story before printing them in the newspaper.

   | 註解 | 證實 (動詞)

560. **Accelerate** (Escalate) the engine when maneuvering a curve to retain control of the car.

   | 註解 | 加速 (動詞)

561. Most men who perform **manual** (physical) labor belong to trade unions.

   | 註解 | 手工的 (形容詞)

562. The **luminous** (radiant) light of the full moon cast an eerie glow over the cottage hidden deep in the forest.

   | 註解 | 光亮的 (形容詞)

563. The confetti thrown from skyscraper fell in **cascades** (torrents) on the parading visitors.

   | 註解 | 洪流 (名詞)

564. The city was crowded with Christmas shoppers **bustling** (bussing) from store to store to buy last-minute gifts.

   | 註解 | 匆忙的 (形容詞)

565. The **drudgery** (labor) of painting every room in the house was relieved by the company of the friends who came to help.

   | 註解 | 苦工 (名詞)

566. The winner of the title **bout** (session) will become the heavyweight boxing champion of the world.

   | 註解 | 一回合，一會期 (名詞)

567. As supplies continued to **dwindle** (lessen), the crash survivors feared they would die of starvation before help arrived.

   | 註解 | 減少 (不定詞)

568. As the fever continued to rise, the child's **delirium** (frenzy) intensified and she called for her mother repeatedly.

   | 註解 | 狂語 (名詞)

569. When you realize the implications of your thoughtless remarks, you will want to **repent** (atone) for having spoken so cruelly to your sister.

   | 註解 | 悔恨，賠罪 (不定詞)

570. "I simply cannot **tolerate** (endure) people who laugh at the mistakes of other", said Jane.

    註解 忍受 (動詞)

571. This special mixture, added to a glass of milk, providers every **nutrient** (sustenance) needed daily by a typical adult to maintain good health.

    註解 營養的 (名詞)

572. When the astronauts landed on the moon, they collected **specimens** (types) of moon soil and rock to bring back to earth.

    註解 標本 (名詞)

573. The poem's meaning was **obscure** (vague), and no one in the class understood it.

    註解 含糊的 (形容詞)

574. Acting on a(n) **impulse** (whim), the woman bought three hats at the sale.

    註解 衝動 (名詞)

575. The original story had been **distorted** (perverted) in the novel because its account lore no similarity to reality.

    註解 扭曲 (動詞，完成被動式)

576. Within the pact year, the bridge **toll** (fee) has been raised from ten cents to a quarter.

    註解 費用，通行費 (名詞)

577. The contractor considered the sloppy work to be a(n) **outrageous** (atrocious) violation of the agreement signed by all the workers.

    註解 憤怒的 (形容詞)

578. Before remodeling the attic, I intend to **insulate** (protect) the walls and ceilings so that the temperature will be more comfortable in both summer and winter.

    註解 隔離，防護 (不定詞)

579. Because he valued his **reputation** (estimation), Larry did not spend time with the boys who were constantly in trouble.

    註解 聲望 (名詞)

580. "Notice the unusual **texture** (weave) of the fabric in the gown", pointed out the saleswoman.

    註解 編織物 (名詞)

581. The President **vetoed** (negated) the bill because he did not think it would
be a good law.

   > 註解　否決 (動詞)

582. You were very **shrewd** (keen) to postpone selling the property until the
price went up.

   > 註解　精明的 (形容詞)

583. When the club decided to allow women to join, the constitution's men-
only provision had to be **amended** (revised).

   > 註解　修改 (動詞，被動式)

584. Although Ed is a pleasant man at home, he runs his office like a **tyrant**
(autocrat).

   > 註解　暴君 (名詞)

585. The new prisoner found life at the work farm so **detestable** (abhorrent)
that he immediately began to plan his escape.

   > 註解　憎恨的 (形容詞)

586. The **homage** (tribute) paid to the three astronauts who first traveled to and
landed on the moon was richly deserved honor and attention.

   > 註解　尊崇 (名詞)

587. The lion **devoured** (consumed) its prey, pulling the flesh from the carcass
in large chunks.

   > 註解　吞食 (動詞)

588. Animals care for their young by **instinct** (tendency) rather than by any
formal instruction.

   > 註解　本能 (名詞)

589. "The drought was such a **calamity** (adversity) to this region that the
settlers moved out and never returned," explained the lecturer.

   > 註解　災難 (名詞)

590. When the famous statesman died, a national day of mourning was
proclaimed (decreed) by the President.

   > 註解　宣布 (動詞，被動式)

591. The ruthless man **degraded** (debased) the boy in front of his friends,
reprimanding him and recalling his past mistakes.

   > 註解　貶低 (動詞)

592. Barry was **reluctant** (loath) to give the commencement address because he did not like the idea of speaking before a large group of people.
　　註解　不願意的 (形容詞)

593. The campers heard a strange **rustling** (movement) in the trees.
　　註解　沙沙聲 (名詞)

594. The hotel manager became suspicious of those people who were **loitering** (loafing).
　　註解　閒蕩 (動詞，進行式)

595. Picasso was a **well-known** (celebrated) cubist painter.
　　註解　著名的 (形容詞)

596. The department chairman refused to authorize the **requisition** (request).
　　註解　要求 (名詞)

597. The counterfeit bills were a good **facsimile** (reproduction) of the real ones.
　　註解　複製 (名詞)

598. The **boundary** (border) between Canada and the United States has been unfortified for over one hundred years.
　　註解　邊界 (名詞)

599. While they were away on vacation, they allowed their mail to **accumulate** (pile up) at the post office.
　　註解　堆積 (不定詞)

600. John's unsportsmanlike behavior caused him to be **ostracized** (shunned) by the other members of the country club.
　　註解　排斥 (不定詞，不定詞被動式)

601. After listening to the testimony, the members of the jury delivered their **verdict** (decision).
　　註解　判斷 (名詞)

602. Nearly half of the town's inhabitants are descendants of **indigenous** (native) civilizations.
　　註解　固有的 (形容詞)

603. After a long lunch hour, business **resumes** (continues) as usual.
　　註解　繼續 (動詞)

604. Under the major's able **leadership** (guidance), the soldiers found safety.
　　註解　響導 (名詞)

605. Larry was so **absorbed** (engrossed) in his novel that he forgot about his dinner cooking in the oven.
註解　專心的 (形容詞)

606. The question was discarded because it was **ambiguous** (vague).
註解　含糊的 (形容詞)

607. The news of the president's death **astonished** (astounded) the world.
註解　令人震驚 (動詞)

608. A **multitude** (huge crowd) of people attended the found- raising presentation in the mall.
註解　群眾 (名詞)

609. Mark cannot talk well because he has a speech **impediment** (defect).
註解　口吃，結巴 (名詞)

610. The **rigor** (severity) exhibited by the general was totally unwarranted.
註解　剛強 (名詞)

611. When he was a director of the company, his first **accomplishment** (achievement) was to bring about better working conditions.
註解　實現 (名詞)

612. The passengers on the boat were **mesmerized** (hypnotized) by the motion of the sea.
註解　迷住 (動詞，被動式)

613. The guests at the lunch enjoyed it very much but refused to eat the **raw** (uncooked) fish.
註解　生的 (形容詞)

614. After a long, hard struggle, we **gradually** (slowly) succeeded in having people accept the truth of our theory.
註解　慢慢地 (副詞)

615. That artist did not achieve acclaim because he was **an imitator** (a copier), not a creator.
註解　模仿者 (名詞)

616. During the war, many foreign lands were **confiscated** (sequestrated) by the government.
註解　沒收 (動詞，被動式)

617. The television station was **inundated** (flooded) with calls protesting the distasteful program.

    註解 淹沒 (動詞，被動式)

618. The fourth years sociology class was a **homogeneous** (uniform) group of university students.

    註解 同類的 (形容詞)

619. The discontented students **retaliated** (took revenge) by boycotting the school cafeteria.

    註解 報復 (動詞)

620. John didn't enjoy the rock concert because he thought the **tempo** (rhythm) was bad.

    註解 節奏 (名詞)

621. Marvin's doctor said he was **obese** (corpulent) and had take immediate measures to correct the problem.

    註解 肥胖的 (形容詞)

622. John's **unabashed** (unembarrassed) behavior caused great concern among his teachers.

    註解 不害臊的 (形容詞)

623. The director's **spacious** (roomy) new office overlooked the city.

    註解 寬廣的 (形容詞)

624. Before the earthquake hit the area, many minor **tremors** (vibrations) were felt.

    註解 震動的 (名詞)

625. Marcia's career involved a **dual** (twofold) role for her as a counselor and a teacher.

    註解 二重的 (形容詞)

626. Sally was **mortified** (humiliated) by her dates unprecedented behavior.

    註解 羞辱 (動詞，被動式)

627. Nothing could **efface** (erase) the people's memory of their former leader's cruelty although many years had elapsed.

    註解 抹滅 (動詞)

628. The protesting crowd **dispersed** (scattered) after the rally.

    註解 解散 (動詞)

629. After the drops were placed in the patient's eyes, his pupils became **dilated** (enlarged).

    註解　擴大的 (形容詞)

630. In that organization, they place **emphasis** (stress) on mutual aid and cooperation.

    註解　強調 (名詞)

631. Jan took many **snapshots** (photos) while on vacation in Europe.

    註解　快照 (名詞)

632. The **daring** (bold) young man rode through the Indian village trying to find his long-lost sister.

    註解　勇敢的 (形容詞)

633. The house by the sea had a mysterious air of **serenity** (calmness) about it.

    註解　寧靜 (名詞)

634. Marsha found it difficult to **cope with** (deal with) the loss of her job.

    註解　負擔 (不定詞)

635. **Migrant** (Transient) workers have difficulty finding steady employment.

    註解　移民 (名詞)

636. The sun's intense rays **distorted** (altered) the image on the horizon.

    註解　扭曲，變更 (動詞)

637. His company **empowered** (authorized) him to negotiate the contract.

    註解　授權 (動詞)

638. The principle **congratulated** (praised) the student on his outstanding display of leadership.

    註解　稱讚 (動詞)

639. **Numbing** (Paralyzing) terror filled their brains as they witnessed the explosions.

    註解　昏迷的 (形容詞)

640. Penny's **impromptu** (extemporaneous) speech given at the state competition won her the first prize.

    註解　即席的 (形容詞)

641. The salon was the most elegant room Madeline had ever seen, despite its **austerity** (simplicity).

    註解　樸素 (名詞)

642. The raccoon is a **nocturnal** (night) animal.

   註解　夜間的 (形容詞)

643. Double agents live in a **perpetual** (constant) state of fear.

   註解　永久的 (形容詞)

644. After receiving the insulting letter, Ron became **furious** (irate).

   註解　狂怒的 (形容詞)

645. If the crop are not **irrigated** (watered) soon, the harvest will be sparse.

   註解　灌溉 (動詞，被動式)

646. The coroner was able to extract a **tiny** (infinitesimal) particle of cloth
   from under the victim's fingernail.

   註解　微小的 (形容詞)

647. The students' records were not readily **accessible** (available) for their
   perusal.

   註解　可達到的 (形容詞)

648. Professor Johnson has a **thorough** (complete) knowledge of Egyptian
   hieroglyphics.

   註解　徹底的 (形容詞)

649. The old utilities building was **demolished** (razed) and a new high-rise
   took its place.

   註解　破壞 (動詞，被動式)

650. The **current** (latest) edition of that magazine discusses the ancient
   civilizations of Latin America.

   註解　最近的 (形容詞)

651. Joyce is loved by all her friends because she is very **congenial** (pleasant).

   註解　意氣相投的 (形容詞)

652. Prehistoric cave art **portrayed** (depicted) animals in motion.

   註解　描繪 (動詞)

653. Victoria Holt and William Shakespeare are **prolific** (productive) writers.

   註解　大量生產的 (形容詞)

654. After the rope had broken, the mountain climber was left **dangling**
   (swinging) freely.

   註解　搖擺 (動詞，進行式)

655. The speaker was asked to **condense** (abbreviate) his presentation in order to allow his audience to ask questions.

> 註解 簡潔，縮短 (不定詞)

656. We were caught in a **deluge** (downpour) while returning from our vacation.

> 註解 傾盆大雨 (名詞)

657. The driver of the car was **liable** (legally responsible) for the damages caused to the passenger.

> 註解 有責任的 (形容詞)

658. The Lucas family **emigrated** (departed) from Switzerland before the war.

> 註解 移居他國 (動詞)

659. We decided to pay for the furniture on the **installment** (monthly payment) plan.

> 註解 分期付款 (名詞)

660. The supervision dictated a **memo** (note) to her secretary.

> 註解 備忘錄 (名詞)

661. It is **imperative** (necessary) that they arrive on time for the lecture.

> 註解 必要的 (形容詞)

662. The professor tried to **stimulate** (encourage) interest in archaeology by taking his students on expeditions.

> 註解 鼓舞 (不定詞)

663. As a result of the accident, the police **revoked** (canceled) his driver's license.

> 註解 取消 (動詞)

664. The children were **frolicking** (running playfully) in the park.

> 註解 嬉戲 (動詞，進行式)

665. Fear of pirate **raids** (invasions) caused the Spaniards to fortify their coastline.

> 註解 侵犯 (名詞)

666. That area of the country is **laced** (crisscrossed) with large and often dangerous rivers.

> 註解 畫十字狀的 (形容詞)

667. Twenty-five percent of Ecuador's population speak Quechua **exclusively** (only).

> 註解 唯一地 (副詞)

668. Having come from a(n) **affluent** (wealthy) society, Dick found it difficult to adjust to a small country town.

註解　富有的 (形容詞)

669. Most students **abhor** (detest) lengthy exams at the end of the year.

註解　痛恨 (動詞)

670. King Mida's **greed** (avarice) led him to spend a life of grief.

註解　貪婪 (名詞)

671. The new building was to be **octagonal** (eight sided) in shape.

註解　八角形的 (形容詞)

672. The people interviewed for the survey were **randomly** (indiscriminately) selected.

註解　隨便地 (副詞)

673. The foreign countries attempt at a **blockade** (closure) of the port was unsuccessful.

註解　封鎖 (名詞)

674. During the American colonial period, the capable leaders **instilled** (implanted).

註解　灌輸 (動詞)

675. Allowing fields to lie **fallow** (unplanted) is one means of restoring fertility.

註解　休耕的 (形容詞)

676. American **legend** (myth) says that Johnny Applessed planted apple orchards throughout Ohio.

註解　傳說 (名詞)

677. The powerful ruler **suppressed** (quashed) a rebellion and punished the instigators.

註解　鎮壓 (動詞)

678. That **vast** (enormous) region was irrigated by the large river and its many tributaries.

註解　廣大的 (形容詞)

679. The dog saw his **reflection** (image) in the pool of water.

註解　反射，影像 (名詞)

680. The tornado caused irreparable (irrecoverable) damage to the Florida citrus crop.

註解　不能挽回的 (形容詞)

681. The spy used a **fictitious** (false) name while dealing with the enemy.
     > 註解　虛構的 (形容詞)

682. The flowers on the table were a **manifestation** (demonstration) of the child's love for his mother.
     > 註解　流露，顯示 (名詞)

683. Frank **condoned** (overlooked) his brother's actions because he knew he meant well.
     > 註解　寬恕 (動詞)

684. Many new medicines today **eradicate** (wipe out) diseases before they become too widespread.
     > 註解　撲滅 (動詞)

685. The thieves were trying to **perpetrate** (commit) a robbery in the office building.
     > 註解　觸犯 (不定詞)

686. When the protestor entered the meeting clad only in a beach towel, the audience was **dumbfounded** (speechless).
     > 註解　啞然失聲的 (形容詞)

687. Andy's **jocular** (jesting) manner made him loved by all his companions.
     > 註解　滑稽的 (形容詞)

688. The student's **wan** (pale) appearance caused the teacher to send him home.
     > 註解　蒼白的 (形容詞)

689. The doctor asked the patient to **disrobe** (undress) before the examination.
     > 註解　脫衣服 (不定詞)

690. Because Dolly is such a good cook, she has **concocted** (created) a great new recipe.
     > 註解　編造 (動詞，完成式)

691. Her **brusque** (abrupt) manner surprised all the guests.
     > 註解　粗率的 (形容詞)

692. She didn't say much, but her tone of voice **insinuated** (suggested) more.
     > 註解　暗示 (動詞)

693. The young couple chose a **secluded** (isolated) place for their picnic.
     > 註解　隔絕的 (形容詞)

694. The victors **defined** (dictated) their teams to the conquered.
     > 註解　指定，認為 (動詞)

695. The speaker **accentuated** (emphasized) the need for cooperation in the
project that we were about to undertake.

> 註解　強調 (動詞)

696. The number of **unemployed** (jobless) people in our country is increasing
rapidly.

> 註解　失業的 (形容詞)

697. Christopher Columbus was the first person to **navigate** (sail) under the
patronage of Queen Isabella of Spain.

> 註解　航行 (不定詞)

698. A new government department was established to control **maritime** (sea)
traffic.

> 註解　海上的 (形容詞)

699. His **involuntary** (automatic) reflexes betrayed his feelings.

> 註解　本能的 (形容詞)

700. A middle-aged woman of tremendous **girth** (rotundity) sat down beside
the other patients in the waiting room.

> 註解　圓胖 (名詞)

701. The atmosphere in the police chief's office was electric with **contention**
(discord).

> 註解　爭論 (名詞)

702. The slender boy **scaled** (climbed) the wall like a lizard.

> 註解　爬越 (動詞)

703. The Royal Museum contains a **facsimile** (copy) of the king's famous
declaration.

> 註解　複製 (名詞)

704. The author wrote with great **clarity** (clearness), not missing a single detail.

> 註解　明晰 (名詞)

705. After the alien spacecraft had hovered over the park for a short while, it
vanished (disappeared).

> 註解　消失 (動詞)

706. Her childhood **poverty** (indigene) caused Lucy to be very thrifty as she
grew older.

> 註解　貧窮 (名詞)

707. While in Europe on vacation, the twins **roamed** (wandered) the countryside on their bikes.

   註解 　閒逛 (動詞)

708. Let's **suppose** (imagine) that we are floating in a cool pool on a hot summer's day.

   註解 　假定 (動詞)

709. The government is engaged in a project to pacify the **hostile** (antagonistic) element of society.

   註解 　敵對的 (形容詞)

710. Recent border **confrontations** (contradictions) between the two military groups lend credence to the rumors an impending war.

   註解 　對立，矛盾 (名詞)

711. The ancient Greek temple is **perched** (located) on top of Athens' highest hill.

   註解 　座落 (動詞，被動式)

712. During the conference, the speaker tried to **convey** (communicate) his feelings concerning the urgency of a favorable decision.

   註解 　傳達 (不定詞)

713. The high mountain climate is cold and **inhospitable** (uninviting).

   註解 　荒涼的 (形容詞)

714. An unsuccessful attempt was made to **salvage** (save) the yacht and its contents.

   註解 　救援 (不定詞)

715. The art students were **enthralled** (captivated) by the sheer beauty of the portrait which hung before them.

   註解 　迷惑 (動詞，被動式)

716. It was difficult to apprehend the criminal because of the **sketchy** (vague) details supplied by the witness.

   註解 　不徹底的 (形容詞)

717. The Titanic lies buried in its **aqueous** (watery) tomb.

   註解 　水的 (形容詞)

718. The scientist tried to **fuse** (unite) the two tubes but found it impossible to do.

   註解 　結合 (不定詞)

719. The recent medical breakthrough was the **culmination** (climax) of many long years of experimentation.

   註解　頂點 (名詞)

720. Few countries today enjoy **prosperous** (flourishing) economics.

   註解　繁榮的 (形容詞)

721. After World War 11, Russia **emerged** (came forth) as a world power.

   註解　出現 (動詞)

722. His replies **were inconsistent with** (contradicted) his previous testimony.

   註解　相反 (動詞片語)

723. Her only chance eludes her **pursuer** (follower) was to mingle with the crowd.

   註解　追隨者 (名詞)

724. The president of the company will **resign** (quit) at the end of the fiscal year.

   註解　辭職 (動詞，未來式)

725. The detective's **resourcefulness** (skill) helped him solve the mystery.

   註解　足智多謀 (名詞)

726. Perhaps the customer has **overlooked** (neglected) his monthly statement and not paid the bill.

   註解　疏忽 (動詞，完成式)

727. John was not promoted because his work did not meet the manager's **expectations** (anticipations).

   註解　預料 (名詞)

728. The students were given **complimentary** (free) passes for the new movie.

   註解　免費的 (形容詞)

729. She discarded the **cores** (centers) after Nillie had baked the apple pie.

   註解　果心 (名詞)

730. After receiving her check, Suzy **endorsed** (signed) it and took it to the bank.

   註解　背書，簽名 (動詞)

731. The professor's **introductory** (preliminary) remarks concerned the development of the laser beam.

   註解　初步的 (形容詞)

732. **Fragments** (Pieces) of the Dead Sea Scrolls have been found in recent years.

   註解　碎片 (名詞)

733. The daring rescue of those stranded on the mountaintop was truly a **creditable** (praiseworthy) deed.

   註解　令人欽佩的 (形容詞)

734. That he should ask her to marry him was rather **presumptuous** (audacious) on his part.

   註解　大膽的 (形容詞)

735. The pianist was **adept** (proficient) at playing the arpeggios.

   註解　精通的 (形容詞)

736. The president's **compassion** (pity) for the refugees caused him to admit a very large number of them.

   註解　同情 (名詞)

737. The **burglar** (thief) broke into the house through the attic.

   註解　盜賊 (名詞)

738. I found the story **incredible** (unbelievable).

   註解　令人不敢相信的 (形容詞)

739. I don't mind giving him things, but he never **does the same in return**. (reciprocates)

   註解　回報 (動詞片語)

740. He checked his composition by reading it **out loud**. (aloud)

   註解　大聲地 (副詞片語)

741. To change a tire, you must **jack up** (elevate) the car.

   註解　提高 (動詞)

742. The milk in these containers is **adulterated**. (spoiled)

   註解　劣質的 (形容詞)

743. How do you describe the **plight** (bad situation) of the oil-hungry nations?

   註解　處境 (名詞)

744. A **typical** (characteristic) color of roses is red.

   註解　典型的 (形容詞)

745. Something is **the matter** (wrong) with my doorbell.

   註解　有點問題 (名詞)

746. Alex knew that he must **breathe** (tell) nothing of this to Nancy.

   註解　說出 (動詞)

747. The group **ridiculed** (laughed at) my suggestion.

   註解　譏笑 (動詞)

748. I hope you are not going to **abandon** (give up completely) your project.

   註解　放棄 (不定詞)

749. The machine has been **out of order** (broken) since last month.

   註解　壞掉的 (形容詞)

750. "I can't **make head or tail of** (understand) this sentence in your essay,"
   said the professor.

   註解　了解 (動詞)

751. The soldier **activated** (detonated) the hand grenade.

   註解　爆裂 (動詞)

752. A superstitious person thinks that a black cat is a bad **omen** (wish).

   註解　預兆 (名詞)

753. She wants to **hitch** (connect) her trailer to your car.

   註解　勾住(定詞)

754. That the army would be defeated was **inevitable** (certain).

   註解　確定的 (形容詞)

755. The motorist was **reproached** (blamed) by the woman trying to cross the
   street.

   註解　譴責 (動詞，被動式)

756. When he remembered the joke, he **chuckled** (laughed quietly).

   註解　偷笑 (動詞)

757. This time I passed the examination, but **the time before** (**last time** I
   didn't.

   註解　上次地 (副詞)

758. Tom is so **jealous** (envious) that he hates his wife to go anywhere without
   hi.

   註解　愛惜的 (形容詞)

759. The 1920's in America were a decade of great **prosperity** (economic
   success).

   註解　繁榮 (名詞)

760. Please **keep in mind** (remember) what I have told you.

   註解 記住 (動詞片語)

761. In a crisis you must **keep your head** (stay calm).

   註解 冷靜 (動詞片語)

762. Ed found the book **enlightening** (illuminating).

   註解 啓發 (動名詞)

763. She follows orders well, but she seldom **initiates** (starts) action.

   註解 開始 (動詞)

764. Tom cannot **afford** (buy) a new bicycle this year.

   註解 負擔 (動詞)

765. We **intended** (planned) to go on vacation then.

   註解 打算 (動詞)

766. This arrangement is only a **tentative** (temporary) one.

   註解 暫時的 (形容詞)

767. Because of its **toxic** (poisonous) condition, the water could not be used.

   註解 有毒的 (形容詞)

768. The forests were dry because of the **dry spell** (drought).

   註解 乾旱時期 (名詞片語)

769. They had such an argument that we thought they would **come to blows** (hit each other).

   註解 毆打 (動詞片語)

770. No, he's not married; he's a **bachelor** (single man).

   註解 單身漢 (名詞)

771. He who **hesitates** (waits) is lost.

   註解 猶豫 (動詞)

772. The judge refused to **release** (free) the prisoner.

   註解 釋放 (不定詞)

773. Everyone says that Jimmy **resembles** (looks like) his father.

   註解 相似 (動詞)

774. My aunt then gave me **a piece of her mind** (her outspoken opinion).

   註解 直話直說 (名詞片語)

775. She's very **foolish** (gullible); she believes anything she's told.

   註解 易受騙的 (形容詞)

776. John **lost his temper** (became angry) and kicked the vending machine.

   註解 暴怒 (動詞片語)

777. Everything must be in perfect order to please Morgan; he's very **fussy** (fastidious).

   註解 挑剔的 (形容詞)

778. The department store clerk was **impudent** (rude).

   註解 魯莽的 (形容詞)

779. The thief **diverted** (turned aside) the old man's attention while he picked his victim's pocket.

   註解 轉移 (動詞)

780. Large cities should try to **eradicate** (eliminate) slum sections.

   註解 根除 (不定詞)

781. Having ice cream in addition to cake would be **a luxury** (an extravagance).

   註解 浪費 (名詞)

782. Charlie can't go to the movie because he's **under age** (too young).

   註解 太年輕 (形容詞片語)

783. **As luck would have it** (Fatefully), Richard was lunching alone that day.

   註解 命運注定地 (副詞片語)

784. "Are you trying to **pull my leg** (deceive me)?" I demanded.

   註解 欺騙 (不定詞片語)

785. Why don't you **talk that over with** (discuss that with) an expert?

   註解 討論 (動詞片語)

786. Over 500 people **took part in** (participated in) the parade.

   註解 參加 (動詞片語)

787. These new tax forms are really **a nuisance**. (an annoyance)

   註解 苦惱 (名詞)

788. The store will give the discount **across the board** (on every item).

   註解 每一樣東西 (介詞片語)

789. Everyone in the office **gave** (donated some money) to the Red Cross.

   註解 捐獻 (動詞)

790. Carlo showed us his **diagram** (sketch) of the machine.

   註解 圖表 (名詞)

791. Few executives are **modest** (humble).

　　註解　有禮貌的 (形容詞)

792. There was quite **a clamor** (a loud noise) when the employees were asked to take pay cuts.

　　註解　紛亂 (名詞)

793. That poem is his most **noteworthy** (remarkable) work.

　　註解　顯著的 (形容詞)

794. Having sold curiosities for years, Comstock was **inured** (accustomed) to the grotesque.

　　註解　習慣的 (形容詞)

795. She went to buy three **traps for mice** (mousetraps).

　　註解　捕鼠器 (名詞片語)

796. Jane had no intention of **playing second fiddle to** (taking a less important position than) Betty.

　　註解　次等 (名詞片語)

797. The judge had a very **sober** (serious) expression on his face.

　　註解　嚴肅的 (形容詞)

798. How many bottles of champagne do you have **on hand** (available)?

　　註解　可利用的 (介詞片語)

799. Please **keep an eye on** (watch) my purse while I telephone.

　　註解　注視，留心 (動詞片語)

800. He was **incapacitated** (disabled) for several months after the accident.

　　註解　不適宜的 (形容詞)

801. Winning the trophy was **an accomplishment** (an achievement).

　　註解　完成 (名詞)

802. Allen **excels at** (is proficient in) music.

　　註解　擅長 (動詞片語)

803. Winston Churchill gave a **moving** (stirring) speech.

　　註解　動人的 (形容詞)

804. Please **enlighten** (instruct) me as to why you did not call me.

　　註解　說明 (動詞)

805. My grandfather was a very **benevolent** (charitable) man.

　　註解　慈善的 (形容詞)

806. Oliver stared **blankly** (absentmindedly) in to the fire.
   註解　茫然地 (副詞)

807. You're **leaving me in the bush** (deserting me).
   註解　遺棄 (動詞，進行式)

808. The wolf in the **untamed** (wild) ancestor of the dog.
   註解　未馴服的 (形容詞)

809. The **matron** (woman superintendent) at the prison refused to speak to the reporters.
   註解　女舍監 (名詞)

810. Joe's illness forced him to **restrict** (limit) his activities.
   註解　限制 (不定詞)

811. Rene is **ignorant** of (uninformed about) world affairs.
   註解　無知的 (形容詞)

812. My employer **hit the ceiling** (became angry) when I was late for work the second time in a week.
   註解　生氣 (動詞片語)

813. The story of Santa Claus is a **myth** (legend) cherished by children.
   註解　神話 (名詞)

814. He likes **country** (hillbilly) music.
   註解　鄉村的，山地的 (形容詞)

815. They **raised a hue and cry** (made a great deal of noise) just outside the gate.
   註解　大聲叫喊 (動詞片語)

816. Peter was the most **garrulous** (talkative) person at the party.
   註解　多嘴的 (形容詞)

817. A **glut** (overabundance) in the oil supply will drive the price of gasoline down.
   註解　大量 (名詞)

818. The remarks that the student made to the teacher were **beside the point** (not related).
   註解　無相關的 (介詞片語)

819. The spy felt **endangered** (threatened) by the man following him.
   註解　危險的 (形容詞)

820. Mary is one of the prettiest girls I have ever **laid eyes on** (seen).

   註解 看過 (動詞，完成式)

821. You must learn to **keep your head** (remain calm) when asked a difficult question on a test.

   註解 冷靜 (不定詞片語)

822. When are you going to **break the news to** (tell) your family?

   註解 告知 (不定詞片語)

823. The reporter refused to **reveal** (make known) the source of his information.

   註解 透露 (不定詞)

824. The Irish countryside is **picturesque** (quaint), dotted with small cottages and cries-crossed by stone fences.

   註解 生動的 (形容詞)

825. Why do you **ridicule** (make fun of) that girl's dress?

   註解 譏笑 (動詞)

826. She was not **thoughtful** (considerate) enough to give the old woman her seat on the bus.

   註解 思慮的 (形容詞)

827. The Iranians did not **see eye to eye** (agree) with the Americans about releasing the hostages.

   註解 同意 (動詞片語)

828. My family is looking for **a condominium** (an individually owned apartment).

   註解 可以自由買賣的公寓 (名詞)

829. The police are looking for a man who is **molesting** (disturbing) young women.

   註解 調戲 (動詞，進行式)

830. The fog was thick that the car ahead of ours was hardly **visible** (obvious).

   註解 顯明的 (形容詞)

831. Let's keep the **delicate** (fragile) vase on a high shelf away from the children.

   註解 精美的，脆弱的 (形容詞)

832. I'd love to have a **hot dog** (frankfurter) on a roll.

   註解 熱狗，香腸 (名詞，同 frankforter)

833. We must be prepared for **substantial** (large)increases in gasoline prices during the coming decade.

   註解 重大的 (形容詞)

834. Mr. Allen **takes a dim view of** (has little confidence in) politics.

   註解 持悲觀 (動詞片語)

835. That apartment has been **vacant** (empty) for over a month.

   註解 淨空的 (形容詞)

836. The game will be **in the bag** (assured) if out pitcher doesn't hurt his arm again.

   註解 確信的 (介詞片語)

837. Ann was so **mixed up** (confused) she could not answer the teacher's question.

   註解 混淆的 (形容詞片語)

838. His mother said, "Smoking will **stunt** (prevent) your growth."

   註解 阻礙 (動詞)

839. A politician who is **corrupt** (dishonest) is not fit to hold office.

   註解 貪污的 (形容詞)

840. There was **pandemonium** (a wild uproar) when the company announced it was cutting wages.

   註解 大混亂 (名詞)

841. We must prevent one person from **mauling** (beating) another.

   註解 虐打 (動名詞)

842. Don't **conceal** (hide) the fact that you are selling a car with bad brakes.

   註解 隱匿 (動詞)

843. He **took on** (assumed) so much work, he had no time for pleasure.

   註解 承擔 (動詞片語)

844. The owner **turned down** (refused) an offer of 50,000 for his house.

   註解 拒絕 (動詞片語)

845. In all my travels, I have never **run across** (discovered) a more beautiful city than San Francisco.

   註解 遇到 (動詞，完成式)

846. Every felt that the referee's decision was **impartial** (fair).

   註解 公平的 (形容詞)

847. She is a person who always **speaks her mind** (gives her frank opinion).

    > 註解 　說坦白 (動詞片語)

848. Young adults must **break away from** (escape from) their parents' control, in order to achieve independence and maturity.

    > 註解 　脫離 (動詞片語)

849. There was **tranquility** (calmness) all about us while we were rowing the boat.

    > 註解 　安靜 (名詞)

850. The **continuous** (non-stop) drumming was driving the tourist mad.

    > 註解 　連續的 (形容詞)

851. Don't **magnify** (enlarge) the problems that you are having with your husband.

    > 註解 　擴大 (動詞)

852. There was **turmoil** (confusion) at the union meeting.

    > 註解 　騷亂 (名詞)

853. His wife chose very **ornate** (elaborate) furniture.

    > 註解 　華麗的 (形容詞)

854. Being well organized is an **asset** (valuable quality) in many areas.

    > 註解 　資產 (名詞)

855. My husband and I would **cherish** (appreciate) a home in the country.

    > 註解 　懷抱 (動詞)

856. Lily **magnified** (enlarged) her problems while she complaining about her bad luck.

    > 註解 　擴大 (動詞)

857. Queen Victoria refused to **relinquish** (give up) the throne to her son Edward.

    > 註解 　放棄 (不定詞)

858. The roses are **exquisite** (very beautiful) this spring.

    > 註解 　精美的 (形容詞)

859. Many people were **injured** (harmed) during the storm.

    > 註解 　受傷的 (形容詞)

860. Most graduate schools are not interested in **run-of-the-mill** (average) students.

    > 註解 　普通 (名詞片語)

861. Mr. Allen was **shaken up** (nervous and upset) by the fake alarm.

   註解　不安的 (形容詞片語)

862. The bow and arrow as a war weapon is now **obsolete** (out of use).

   註解　落伍的 (形容詞)

863. Maria travels **back and fort**h (frequently) between Miami and New York.

   註解　經常地 (副詞片語)

864. A **pretentious** (showy) person is usually disliked.

   註解　虛偽的 (形容詞)

865. The parade **retarded** (slowed up) the progress of the traffic going

   crosstown.

   註解　阻礙 (動詞)

866. The tiny flowers are **delicate** (fragile).

   註解　脆弱的 (形容詞)

867. Try to read phrase by phrase, not **word by word** (one word at a time).

   註解　逐字 (名詞片語)

868. That doesn't make sense; I think your reasoning is **fallacious** (faulty).

   註解　有缺點的 (形容詞)

869. After much discussion, we decided to **retain** (keep) the present system.

   註解　保持 (不定詞)

870. Marianne **looks up to** (admires) her older brother.

   註解　尊敬 (動詞片語)

871. The **plates** (dishes) are warming in the oven.

   註解　盤食 (名詞)

872. In bringing me up, my parents always tried to **stress** (emphasize) the

   importance of honesty.

   註解　強調 (不定詞)

873. They were both angry, so their argument was **very bitter** (acrimonious).

   註解　尖刻的 (形容詞片語)

874. The cigarette machine **dispenses** (gives out) matches too.

   註解　分發 (動詞)

875. The Chief Justice is an **important** (eminent) figure in America.

   註解　崇高的 (形容詞)

876. There are many influences that **debase** (lower) the value of the dollar.

   註解　貶低 (動詞)

877. Only nasty characters would **trample on** (step heavily on) these once beautiful flower beds.

   註解 　踐踏 (動詞片語)

878. Professor Jones is **a colleague** (an associate) of Professor Allen.

   註解 　同事 (名詞)

879. If Barry has any time **left over** (by the clock), he will help me with my French lesson.

   註解 　剩下地 (副詞片語)

880. Joe was **careless** (negligent) and caused the accident.

   註解 　疏忽的 (形容詞)

881. Yoko enjoys telling jokes and stories at **informal** (casual) gatherings.

   註解 　偶然的 (形容詞)

882. Mayor Kock **commended** (praised) Detective Darin for his bravery.

   註解 　稱讚 (動詞)

883. When you are young, you take more **risks** (chances) without worrying.

   註解 　風險 (名詞)

884. Everyone wanted me to agree, but I **stood my ground** (maintained my position).

   註解 　堅持立場 (動詞片語)

885. I never know what he means; he speaks so **vaguely** (equivocally).

   註解 　含混地 (副詞)

886. Josephine **must have forgotten** (is due to forget) her books, for they are still here.

   註解 　想必忘了 (動詞片語)

887. His aloofness **mystifies** (puzzles) many.

   註解 　迷惑 (動詞)

888. The mothers of the war heroes **grieved** (wept) for their lost sons.

   註解 　悲傷 (動詞)

889. We're in a **muddle** (confused mess) because we missed our plane.

   註解 　一團亂 (名詞)

890. A politic **fanatic** (zealot), he has fought with revolutionaries all over the world.

   註解 　狂熱 (名詞)

891. Bruce will l**et me use** (lend me) his car tonight.
   > 註解　借給我 (動詞片語)

892. I can hardly believe it; it's **amazing** (incredible).
   > 註解　難以相信的 (形容詞)

893. The politician's voting record proved a great **liability** (handicap) when he ran for re-election.
   > 註解　不利地位，障礙 (名詞)

894. Some of the **regulations** (rules) seemed too severe.
   > 註解　規則 (名詞)

895. Judy **ran across** (happened to meet) an old friend today.
   > 註解　偶然相遇 (動詞片語)

896. The snake turned out to be quite **harmless** (safe).
   > 註解　無害的 (形容詞)

897. He's a real **liar** (hypocrite); he never doses what he says.
   > 註解　騙子 (名詞)

898. Elizabeth **found out** (determined) why the Spanish class was canceled.
   > 註解　發現 (動詞片語)

899. Winters easily **disproved** (refute) Jackson's accusations.
   > 註解　反駁 (動詞)

900. The movie star signed a **lucrative** (profitable) contract.
   > 註解　待遇好的 (形容詞)

901. The real estate broker **goaded** (urged) the couple to put down a deposit.
   > 註解　鼓動 (動詞)

902. We had a lovely visit because the Amorys are so **friendly** (hospitable).
   > 註解　友善的 (形容詞)

903. Because Charles had forgotten his key, he was **locked out** (unable to get in).
   > 註解　被鎖在外 (動詞，被動式)

904. To prevent the dog from running away, his owner **restrained** (tied) him.
   > 註解　監禁 (動詞)

905. Homosexual relationships between men were quite **prevalent** (widespread) in ancient Greece.
   > 註解　流行的 (形容詞)

906. A doctor's handwriting is often **illegible** (hard to read).

  註解 不易閱讀的 (形容詞)

907. The senator received an **anonymous** (an unsigned) letter.

  註解 匿名的 (形容詞)

908. Our company has been **exporting** (sending out of the country for sale) fine wines for one hundred years.

  註解 出口 (動詞，被動進行式)

909. The temptation to **consult** (discuss the matter with) his chief was great.

  註解 商談 (不定詞)

910. The city will be **stifling** (hot) this week.

  註解 窒息的，炎熱的 (形容詞)

911. We stared in **awe** (respect) at the president himself.

  註解 敬畏 (名詞)

912. The wealthy widow was **wary of** (watchful for) swindlers out to fool her.

  註解 小心的 (形容詞片語)

913. The woman's **sallow** (yellowish) skin indicated that she spent little time outdoors.

  註解 灰黃的 (形容詞)

914. Self-denial is one of their **tenets** (doctrines).

  註解 信條 (名詞)

915. Lucille has been feeling **under the weather** (ill).

  註解 生病的 (介詞片語)

916. He hid in the barn for a week after he **escaped** (ran away).

  註解 逃跑 (動詞)

917. My human sexuality instructor agreed to answer questions, providing they were **relevant** (pertinent) to the class.

  註解 關連的 (形容詞)

918. Anna has collection of **miniature** (very small) dolls.

  註解 微小的 (形容詞)

919. Rain at this time of year is quite **abnormal** (unusual).

  註解 不正常的 (形容詞)

920. John is hard to argue with because he likes to **split hairs** (make distinctions that aren't important).

  註解 找細微之事，挑剔 (不定詞片語)

921. Harry **tossed up his chin** (gestured) toward heaven.

   註解 表示 (動詞片語)

922. The rally will **take place** (be held) between the football and the science building.

   註解 舉行 (動詞片語)

923. If you can't **take orders** (follow directions) you'll never learn to give them.

   註解 指令 (動詞片語)

924. The child's fever **receded** (went down) after he had taken the medicine.

   註解 減退 (動詞)

925. Letting the lady sit first at the table is the **conventional** (usual) thing to do.

   註解 傳統的 (形容詞)

926. Robert asked Nancy to keep him **company** (to accompany him).

   註解 同夥 (名詞)

927. Arnold is **a master of** (very good at) comedy.

   註解 精通的 (形容詞片語)

928. We tried hard, but finally we had to **give up** (abandon the attempt).

   註解 放棄 (不定詞片語)

929. Mike really knows how to **call a spade** (be outspoken).

   註解 坦白 (不定詞片語)

930. He wants to **explore** (study) the question more thoroughly before making a decision.

   註解 研究 (不定詞)

931. Where did you get that **ridiculous** (absurd) hat?

   註解 可笑的 (形容詞)

932. I felt very **ambivalent** (torn) about the job offer.

   註解 矛盾的，受傷的 (形容詞)

933. The yellowlegs **is native to** (comes from) that region.

   註解 出產 (動詞片語)

934. We cannot **purse** (learn more about) that subject without guidance.

   註解 支配 (動詞)

935. Marjorie **offered** (gave) a silly excuse.

   註解 提供 (動詞)

936. **Charity** (Deserving respect) is an important quality for a leader.

   註解　博愛 (名詞)

937. His stomach **protruded** (projected) when he wore loose trousers.

   註解　凸出的 (形容詞)

938. Aunt Esther's voice is as clear as **ever** (it always was).

   註解　永遠地 (副詞)

939. Don't listen to that **lovesick** (sentimental) song.

   註解　感傷的 (形容詞)

940. I'm **famished** (hungry), let's eat.

   註解　飢餓的 (形容詞)

941. Although the baseman and the umpire are good friends, they do not

   always **see eye to eye** (agree).

   註解　同意 (動詞片語)

942. For homework Tommy had to do a **complicated** (complex) math problem.

   註解　複雜的 (形容詞)

943. Be careful with that lamp; it is **fragile** (breakable).

   註解　易破的 (形容詞)

944. King Henry VIII rejected the **doctrines** (tenets) of the Catholic Church.

   註解　教條 (名詞)

945. Steven cannot speak; he is **mute** (dumb).

   註解　啞的 (形容詞)

946. He does not **hold back** (restrain) his sarcasm.

   註解　克制 (動詞片語)

947. If only our **dreams** (wishes) could come true?

   註解　夢想 (名詞)

948. After the theft, two employees came under **scrutiny** (investigation).

   註解　詳查 (名詞)

949. Though Helen is **diminutive** (small), she is not shy.

   註解　小的 (形容詞)

950. Geraldine **never fails to read** (always reads) the comics.

   註解　常讀 (動詞片語)

951. Mr. White plays a character of enormous **affability** (pleasantness).

   註解　溫柔 (名詞)

952. The dancers **spun** (whirled) away from us.

    註解 旋轉 (動詞)

953. **Timid** (Shy) people are often overlooked at parties and other social gatherings.

    註解 害羞的 (形容詞)

954. He is the most **obstinate** (stubborn) child I have ever seen.

    註解 固執的 (形容詞)

955. The singer gave a **brilliant** (magnificent) performance.

    註解 亮麗的 (形容詞)

956. Although my grandmother is old and **frail** (weak), she still enjoys cards and listening to dance tunes.

    註解 衰弱的 (形容詞)

957. Every businessman is interested in any **lucrative** (profitable) deal.

    註解 可獲利的 (形容詞)

958. According to the astronomer's **calculations** (figures), Haley's comet will pass over before the end of the century.

    註解 估計 (名詞)

959. Children who come from **deprived** (without funds) families are frequently poor readers.

    註解 剝奪的，使不能的 (形容詞)

960. The salesman **acknowledged** (admitted) that he could have been more courteous.

    註解 承認 (動詞)

961. When I told you that I was very rich, that was a **jest** (joke).

    註解 玩笑 (名詞)

962. That nurse was **delinquent** (neglectful) in giving the patients their medicine on schedule.

    註解 過失的 (形容詞)

963. The beggar **solicited** (requested) passers-by for money.

    註解 請求 (動詞)

964. The child on the street corner is very **insolent** (rude).

    註解 粗野的 (形容詞)

965. If a driver violates the speed limit, he must be prepared to **face the music** (accept the consequences).

   註解 面對結果 (不定詞片語)

966. The enemy ship was **seized** (captured) as it entered the port.

   註解 沒收 (動詞，被動式)

967. There was a **swarm** (great crowd) of children on the playground.

   註解 群眾 (名詞)

968. Let me **urge** (persuade) you to attend the next meeting of the International Students' Association.

   註解 催促 (動詞)

969. The lose of his toy **aroused** (excited) the child's anger.

   註解 引起 (動詞)

970. As chairman, you will have to **delegate** (assign) responsibility to each of the committee members.

   註解 委託 (不定詞)

971. Harry **kept his word** (kept his promise) about paying me the ten dollars that I had lent him.

   註解 答應 (動詞片語)

972. The teacher was **afflicted** (injured) by the fact that several students failed the test.

   註解 難過的 (形容詞)

973. The security guard **ejected** (expelled) two men who were yelling in the courtroom.

   註解 逐出 (動詞)

974. When labor troubles are expected, look for **slump** (decline) in the market.

   註解 景氣 (名詞)

975. **Stealthily** (Slyly), the burglar climbed to the second story window.

   註解 悄悄地 (副詞)

976. The captain decided to **abandon** (leave) the sinking ship.

   註解 放棄 (不定詞)

977. The factory workers' wages were **reduced** (lowered) after they joined the picket line.

   註解 減少 (動詞，被動式)

978. Fred **made a point of phoning** (insisted upon phoning).

　　　註解　堅持觀點 (動詞片語)

979. Many people don't have the **means** (wealth) to buy a home.

　　　註解　財富 (名詞)

980. The refugees **consumed** (devoured) the rice and asked for more.

　　　註解　貪食 (動詞)

981. If you like a **frigid** (very cold) climate, don't go to Florida.

　　　註解　嚴寒的 (形容詞)

982. The movement of troops into Afghanistan is **ominous** (menacing).

　　　註解　脅迫的 (形容詞)

983. The typist **dashed off** (did the job fast) the letter because she had to leave the office early.

　　　註解　急速 (動詞片語)

984. The patient showed **animation** (liveliness) when the doctor said she was improving.

　　　註解　鼓舞 (名詞)

985. In our relationship, we should have the **concept** (thought) of fairness.

　　　註解　概念 (名詞)

986. An intelligent person has no **bias** (prejudice) in matters of race, color, or creed.

　　　註解　偏見 (名詞)

987. The young man visits his mother **every once in a while** (occasionally).

　　　註解　經常地 (副詞片語)

988. I hope to **get to** (arrive at) Los Angeles by noon.

　　　註解　到達 (不定詞片語)

989. The voters are responsible for electing a President who can **govern** (direct) the country intelligently and imaginatively.

　　　註解　統治 (動詞)

990. The dancer's movements appeared **effortless** (easy).

　　　註解　不費力的 (形容詞)

991. She will be **on pins and needles** (very anxious) until the baby is born.

　　　註解　不安的 (介詞片語)

992. The doctor was forced to **postpone** (put off) his vacation because so many of his patients were ill.

　　註解　延期 (不定詞)

993. The man **vanished** (disappeared) when the policeman appeared.

　　註解　消失的 (形容詞)

994. The smoke from the factory **contaminated** (spoiled) the milk.

　　註解　污染 (動詞)

995. Many city dwellers would be **better off** (happier) living in the suburbs.

　　註解　比較快樂的 (形容詞片語)

996. Borg was very **agile** (lively) in winning his tennis match.

　　註解　敏捷的 (形容詞)

997. One of the most brightly colored insects is a **butterfly** (lepidopteron).

　　註解　蝴蝶，有羽翼的昆蟲 (名詞)

998. A new **civic** (municipal) auditorium was built for the citizens.

　　註解　市民的 (形容詞)

999. The **electricity** (electric current) from the dynamo gave the plant power to run its machines.

　　註解　電力 (名詞)

1000. Jim injured his leg in the automobile **accident** (misadventure).

　　註解　災難 (名詞)

1001. A **syllable** (segment of speech) is a section of a word and always contains a vowel sound.

　　註解　音節 (名詞)

1002. The **mileage** (extent) is the distance traveled in miles between two points.

　　註解　哩程 (名詞)

1003. Many wool **fabrics** (fibers) are heavy.

　　註解　布料 (名詞)

1004. The machine was **automatic** (involuntary) and only needed someone to turn the switch.

　　註解　自動的 (形容詞)

1005. A new car **depreciates** (decries) rapidly in the first year.

　　註解　跌價 (動詞)

1006. Many people still use the word "**vehicle**" (conveyance) instead of automobile.

> 註解　交通工具 (名詞)

1007. Jim was **vaccinated** (inoculated) for smallpox.

> 註解　種痘，打疫苗 (動詞，被動式)

1008. The **scent** (odor) of Jean's perfume was aromatic.

> 註解　氣味 (名詞)

1009. Mary had a **fancy** (fantasy) for the party.

> 註解　幻想 (名詞)

1010. The **distribution** (placement) of the work seemed unfair.

> 註解　分配 (名詞)

1011. Bill had a small **splinter** (sliver) of wood in his hand.

> 註解　裂片 (名詞)

1012. All words contain **vowels** (speech sounds).

> 註解　母音 (名詞)

1013. The sign **prohibited** (interdicted) the group from walking further.

> 註解　禁止 (動詞)

1014. The Statue of Liberty is a **permanent** (invariable) reminder of freedom in the United States.

> 註解　永久不變的 (形容詞)

1015. It seemed **risky** (perilous) for Joe to climb the tower alone.

> 註解　危險的 (形容詞)

1016. The speech was long, and Barbara was **bored** (fatigued).

> 註解　疲乏的 (形容詞)

1017. The men just finished the cement work on the street **curb** (curbstone).

> 註解　路邊欄 (名詞)

1018. We **advise** (admonish) you to dress neatly for your interview.

> 註解　勸告 (動詞)

1019. **Alcohol** (Spirits of wine) can be harmful to your body.

> 註解　酒精類 (名詞)

1020. The wide **highway** (main road) led us west.

> 註解　幹道 (名詞)

1021. The car was not of **superior** (higher) quality.

> 註解　較好的 (形容詞)

1022. John and Mary's **divorce** (disunion) was a tragic event.

> 註解　離婚 (名詞)

1023. Jim's boss put **pressure** (oppress) on him to get his work completed.

> 註解　壓力 (名詞)

1024. The **Constitution** (Formation) gives us our basic outline of government.

> 註解　憲法構造 (名詞)

1025. Because Betty did not agree with what Jean had said, there was a **misunderstanding** (discord) between them.

> 註解　不一致 (名詞)

1026. All of Jane's cooking **utensils** (tools) were new.

> 註解　用具 (名詞)

1027. Because of his training, Arvin will **qualify** (adapt) for the job.

> 註解　勝任 (動詞)

1028. It was a **temporary** (transient) lay-off from the factory.

> 註解　暫時的 (形容詞)

1029. Sara gave an **explanation** (elucidation) for being late to work.

> 註解　說明 (名詞)

1030. We will **furnish** (deck out) the living room first with a sofa and two chairs.

> 註解　布置 (動詞)

1031. Ron was **remodeling** (renovating) the living room by painting and adding new doors.

> 註解　整修 (動詞，進行式)

1032. He is **blind** (irrational) to the faults of others.

> 註解　盲目的 (形容詞)

1033. Betty will attempt to **stretch** (draw out) her food allowance so it will last until the end of the week.

> 註解　擴張 (不定詞)

1034. The **number** (digit) attending the party was thirty-two.

> 註解　號碼 (名詞)

1035. The **harvesting** (reaping) of crops usually occurs in the late summer.

> 註解　收穫 (動名詞)

1036. A fringe **benefit** (advantage) is payment other that wages, such as a vacation or insurance.

註解　福利 (名詞)

1037. The hospital had the "**sanitary**" (unpolluted) look.

註解　衛生的 (形容詞)

1038. A city is divided into small **precincts** (wards), or areas, to make it easy for citizens to get to the voting places.

註解　區域 (名詞)

1039. An **incumbent** (A holder) is a person who is in office.

註解　值班 (名詞)

1040. To **register** (enroll) is to have your name put on the list of those eligible to vote.

註解　註冊 (不定詞)

1041. A statement of the goals and policies of a political party is a **platform** (program).

註解　政綱 (名詞)

1042. People who run for public office are called **candidates** (candidatures).

註解　候選人 (名詞)

1043. A **ballot** (vote) is the paper on which a vote is marked.

註解　選票 (名詞)

1044. Lime, sand, and water mixed together make one kind of **plaster** (composition).

註解　組合物 (名詞)

1045. The wedding was the **climax** (acme) of many days of preparation.

註解　高潮 (名詞)

1046. To work the problem, you must **subtract** (deduct).

註解　扣除 (動詞)

1047. The **inspector** (superintendent) approved John's work.

註解　管理者 (名詞)

1048. Our **government** (administration) is democratic.

註解　政府 (名詞)

1049. I am a **citizen** (inhabitant) of the United States.

註解　公民，居民 (名詞)

1050. George Washington loved his country and was among our first great **patriots** (country supporters).

註解 愛國者 (名詞)

1051. Some cookware is made of **aluminum** (aluminium).

註解 鋁 (名詞)

1052. Abe Lincoln had very high **principles** (canons) of honesty and integrity.

註解 原則 (名詞)

1053. He likes to **express** (set forth) his feelings.

註解 表達 (不定詞)

1054. This problem would **baffle** (frustrate) anyone.

註解 困惑 (動詞)

1055. The **climate** (weather) of southern California is warm in the winter.

註解 氣候 (名詞)

1056. The **casserole** (mixture) had meat and vegetables cooked together.

註解 砂鍋菜 (名詞)

1057. A **detergent** (purging agent) will often clean better than soap.

註解 洗潔劑 (名詞)

1058. The **garbage** (trash) truck came around every Monday.

註解 垃圾 (名詞)

1059. The factory had a tall **chimney** (smoke tube).

註解 煙囪 (名詞)

1060. The **pictures** (photographs) on the walls were by a famous artist.

註解 圖畫 (名詞)

1061. Will your **separate** (sunder) the two boys who are fighting?

註解 分開 (動詞)

1062. The mother ran down the steps to **embrace** (hug) her son.

註解 擁抱 (不定詞)

1063. The **raccoon** (nocturnal animal) was killed by a car.

註解 浣熊 (名詞，夜間動物)

1064. A **basin** (wasting container) is a shallow pan and can be of any color.

註解 盤，盆之類 (名詞)

1065. The **manicurist** (manicure) works in a beauty shop.

註解 修指甲師 (名詞)

1066. He had **respect** (estimation) for the new manager.

   註解　敬重 (名詞)

1067. Under **Communism** (a special theory), the government owns and operates all business.

   註解　共產主義 (名詞)

1068. They showed **reverence** (veneration) at his friend's funeral.

   註解　崇敬 (名詞)

1069. He was known for his **neutrality** (neutral status) on the proposition.

   註解　中立 (名詞)

1070. The sun will **blister** (raise blisters) a tender skin.

   註解　生水泡 (動詞)

1071. **Scouring** (Rubbing) a pot is easy with cleanser.

   註解　擦洗 (動名詞)

1072. The doctor gave a **prescription** (medical direction) for medicine which was to be filled at the drug store.

   註解　處方 (名詞)

1073. Most auto accident victims are taken to the **emergency** (extremity) room of the hospital.

   註解　緊急 (名詞)

1074. Doing daily **exercise** (calisthenics) keeps one healthy.

   註解　運動 (名詞)

1075. They are **sociable** (companionable) people and love to give parties.

   註解　愛交際的 (形容詞)

1076. Joe collected bugs for his **biology** (science of living matter) class.

   註解　生物學 (名詞)

1077. He lost **contact** (junction) with his buddy.

   註解　連絡 (名詞)

1078. The girl treated the visitor **snobbishly** (condescendingly).

   註解　勢利眼地 (副詞)

1079. The baseball team was **disqualified** (incapacitated) in the finals.

   註解　取消資格 (動詞，被動式)

1080. The first Edison **phonograph** (gramophone) had a large horn as a speaker.

   註解　留聲機 (名詞)

1081. Police are law **enforcement** (support) officers.

　　　註解　執行 (名詞)

1082. The **assessor** (advisor) appraises our property for tax purposes.

　　　註解　稅務員 (名詞)

1083. Our **representatives** (deputies) in government are chosen by election.

　　　註解　代表 (名詞)

1084. It is wise to **undercoat** (paint) cars in the north to protect them from the salt on the streets.

　　　註解　塗漆 (不定詞)

1085. The patient was in **agonizing** (distressing) pain.

　　　註解　煩惱的 (形容詞)

1086. She **tormented** (hectored) her mother by staying out late every night.

　　　註解　折磨 (動詞)

1087. **Conservation** (Preservation) of water is necessary because of the increased use of water.

　　　註解　儲存 (名詞)

1088. The **equator** (great circle) is an imaginary circle around the globe, dividing the north from the south.

　　　註解　赤道 (名詞)

1089. Green vegetables **enrich** (supply) a diet of meat and potatoes.

　　　註解　補充 (動詞)

1090. Children have much **energy** (power) and want to play most of the time.

　　　註解　活力 (名詞)

1091. Good **nutrition** (nutriment) means you are eating the right food your body needs.

　　　註解　營養品 (名詞)

1092. Milk is **pasteurized** (pasteurized), using heat, to kill germs.

　　　註解　高熱殺菌 (動詞，被動式)

1093. When milk is treated so that the cream will not separate, it is **homogenized** (emulsified).

　　　註解　乳狀的 (形容詞)

1094. **Parliamentary** (Formal) procedure was used to conduct the meeting.

　　　註解　議院的 (形容詞)

1095. The gun happened to have a **cartridge** (cartouche) left in it.

   註解　彈藥筒 (名詞)

1096. Wanda presented her **passbook** (bankbook) to the teller at the bank when she made her car payment.

   註解　存摺 (名詞)

1097. The **tricycle** (velocipede) was broken, and Jimmy was feeling discouraged.

   註解　三輪腳踏車 (名詞)

1098. **Communication** (Imparting thought) is the exchange of ideas or information.

   註解　通知 (名詞)

1099. A **jet** (shooting steam) airplane can fly faster that the speed of sound.

   註解　噴射 (名詞)

1100. The **amusement** (entertainment) park had many unusual rides for fun.

   註解　娛樂 (名詞)

1101. The fence was **barrier** (palisade) between the backyards.

   註解　界線，柵欄 (名詞)

1102. The **rocket** (tube like device) was fired toward the moon.

   註解　火箭 (名詞)

1103. Max will **demonstrate** (illustrate) how to use the machine.

   註解　說明 (動詞)

1104. The **propeller** (propellant) whirled, and the plane started down the runway.

   註解　螺旋槳 (名詞，同 prollent)

1105. The tree-lined **boulevard** (concourse) was beautiful.

   註解　林蔭大道，聚集 (名詞)

1106. The boss trusted Tom with **confidential** (restricted) information because he knew he would not tell it to anyone else.

   註解　祕密的 (形容詞)

1107. The elephant was **enormous** (gigantic).

   註解　巨大的 (形容詞)

1108. She received a large sum of money for her **professional** (occupational) performances.

   註解　職業的 (形容詞)

1109. She was always **borrowing** (obtaining with the promise) something from her neighbors.

   註解　借入 (動詞，進行式)

1110. He seemed to have a **lifetime** (life period) of good luck.

   註解　終身 (名詞)

1111. Many trees are **hollow** (empty) and are fine for squirrels to hide in.

   註解　空心的 (形容詞)

1112. The tree looked so **sturdy** (robust) one would not believe it would fall.

   註解　強壯的 (形容詞)

1113. There are four major bodies of water in the world: the Atlantic, Pacific, Arctic, and Indian **Oceans** (vast seas).

   註解　海洋 (名詞)

1114. He was **honest** (incorruptible), therefore you could depend upon him to tell the truth.

   註解　廉潔的 (形容詞)

1115. He **twisted** (intertwined) the rope to make it stronger.

   註解　纏繞 (動詞)

1116. The cool **beverage** (drink) tasted good in the warm weather.

   註解　飲料 (名詞)

1117. The coffee bubbled noisily in the **percolator** (coffee pot).

   註解　咖啡壺 (名詞)

1118. The **conservation** (supervision) department guards our forests.

   註解　森林保護，管理 (名詞)

1119. We left the island and went over to the **mainland** (principal land).

   註解　大陸 (名詞)

1120. The little boy was put into the **guardianship** (responsibility) of his grandparents for care.

   註解　保護，任務 (名詞)

1121. All the passengers **disembarked** (landed) from the ship and spent the afternoon on shore.

   註解　登岸 (動詞)

1122. The continual rebirth of physical life on earth symbolized the **eternity** (timelessness) of spiritual life.

   註解　永恆 (名詞)

1123. The seek physical, emotional **compatibility** (harmony).

   註解　和平共存 (名詞)

1124. The rising **tide** (current) flooded the lowlands with salt water.

   註解　海潮 (名詞)

1125. Birds singing in the treetops made a joyous **melody** (harmony).

   註解　旋律 (名詞)

1126. A **tempest** (snowstorm) raged in fury across the winter landscape.

   註解　暴風雪或雨 (名詞)

1127. A **tornado** (windstorm) whirled across the land causing widespread destruction.

   註解　龍捲風 (名詞)

1128. The **amphitheater** (arena) was the scene of great plays.

   註解　競技場 (名詞)

1129. The large **buttress** (prop) was built against the wall for support.

   註解　支撐 (名詞)

1130. The artist **dabbled** (worked) here and there on the canvas with different colors of paint.

   註解　涉獵 (動詞)

1131. The old **galley** (rowboat) was a ship that had many oars.

   註解　划船 (名詞)

1132. We started the engine on the **launch** (large boat) and went down the river to Chicago.

   註解　大艇 (名詞)

1133. We had a **conversation** (colloquy) with the president and talked for fifteen minutes.

   註解　談話 (名詞)

1134. The distance one can travel in space is **infinite** (unbounded).

   註解　無限的 (形容詞)

1135. A poor carpenter would build an **inferior** (lower) house.

   註解　較低的 (形容詞)

1136. They **dumped** (unloaded), the wheat into the hopper.

   註解　傾倒 (動詞)

1137. The mayor is a **prominent** (manifest) citizen.

   註解　著名的 (形容詞)

1138. The White House is the **residence** (domicile) of the President.
    > 註解　住所 (名詞)

1139. A **hybrid** (mongrel) plant can be produced by crossing two kinds of plants.
    > 註解　雜種的 (形容詞)

1140. The birthday cake was **resplendent** (gleaming) with candles.
    > 註解　光輝的 (形容詞)

1141. Very old people are often **infirm** (feeble).
    > 註解　微弱的 (形容詞)

1142. The cat and the dog were **incompatible** (unsuitable)
    > 註解　不能共存的 (形容詞)

1143. The use of English in the Mass is an **innovation** (alteration) in America.
    > 註解　改革 (名詞)

1144. The boy was filled with **resentment** (dudgeon) because the teacher had spanked him.
    > 註解　憤恨 (名詞)

1145. The little book is a **condensation** (abridgment) of the big book.
    > 註解　濃縮 (名詞)

1146. The lawyer's speech was so hard to understand it was incomprehensible (not understandable).
    > 註解　不能理解的 (形容詞)

1147. The two leading teams played **opposite** (antagonist) each other in the bowling tournament.
    > 註解　敵手，對抗 (名詞)

1148. A thing that is not real is an **imitation** (a counterfeit).
    > 註解　仿冒 (名詞)

1149. The **lighthouse** (light tower) that aided ships to find their destination was destroyed by the storm.
    > 註解　燈塔 (名詞)

1150. A **million** (thousand times one thousand) dollars is a lot of money.
    > 註解　百萬 (名詞)

1151. There were **crowds** (hordes) of people at the fair.
    > 註解　群眾 (名詞)

1152. The dog chased **rapidly** (fleetly) after the cat.

> 註解 迅速地 (副詞)

1153. An **encyclopedia** (A comprehensive book) is a book which gives us information on many topics.

> 註解 百科全書 (名詞)

1154. The dress she bought had **style** (fashion).

> 註解 流行 (名詞)

1155. The gravel road was **rough** (bumpy).

> 註解 崎嶇不平的 (形容詞)

1156. The desk had a smooth **surface** (outer face).

> 註解 表面 (名詞)

1157. The giraffe at the zoo was an **unusual** (rare) sight for the children.

> 註解 稀奇的 (形容詞)

1158. His **estate** (possession), made up of all his property, was left to his son.

> 註解 房地產 (名詞)

1159. The **mosquito** (dipterous insect) is an insect which breeds in wet and warm places.

> 註解 蚊子 (名詞)

1160. It was **cruel** (ferocious) to beat the child so often.

> 註解 殘忍的 (名詞)

1161. The sick child responded quickly to **treatment** (management).

> 註解 治療 (名詞)

1162. The doctor was a **specialist** (expert) in the field internal medicine.

> 註解 專家 (名詞)

1163. Many southern mansions are built with **pillars** (pilasters) across the front.

> 註解 柱子 (名詞)

1164. The **threat** (menace) of disinheritance caused him to obey his father's wishes.

> 註解 威脅 (名詞)

1165. His **longing** (desire) to go home was fulfilled.

> 註解 願望 (名詞)

1166. She has many qualities of **leadership** (leading ability).

> 註解 領導力 (名詞)

1167. Is there a **possibility** (feasibleness) that you may not come?

    註解　可能性 (名詞，同 feasibility)

1168. The **clergyman** (churchman) spent many years in school training for his vocation.

    註解　牧師，教士 (名詞)

1169. One will **suffer** (endure) pain with a headache.

    註解　遭受 (動詞)

1170. The high **spirit** (essence) of the horse was broken.

    註解　精髓 (名詞)

1171. There are many kinds of **envelopes** (envelops) for mailing purposes.

    註解　信封 (名詞)

1172. He will **deposit** (hoard) his savings in the bank.

    註解　貯存 (動詞)

1173. The applicant for the job had an **interview** (conversation) with Mr. Brown.

    註解　面談 (名詞)

1174. Morse Code is a system of sending messages using **dots and dashes** (signs).

    註解　符號 (名詞片語)

1175. The **inner** (interior) lining of a winter coat is of heavy material.

    註解　內部的 (名詞)

1176. A well-known man often writes his **autobiography** (account) after his retirement.

    註解　自傳 (名詞)

1177. The house is **vacant** (unoccupied) and for sale.

    註解　清空的 (名詞)

1178. We improve our writing with **practice** (operation).

    註解　練習 (名詞)

1179. His **complaint** (faultfinding) about the poor food was sent to the manager.

    註解　挑剔 (名詞)

1180. She went to the **dentist** (tooth curer) to have her teeth filled.

    註解　牙醫師 (名詞)

1181. It took many kinds of **materials** (substances) to stock the new store.

　註解　物質 (名詞)

1182. The company **guaranteed** (insured) their product for one year.

　註解　保證 (動詞)

1183. The books are **published** (issued) in Chicago.

　註解　印刷出版 (動詞，被動式)

1184. We had practically reached our goal by **sun down** (sunset).

　註解　日落地 (副詞片語)

1185. Look for a job in the **classified** (various) advertisements in your paper.

　註解　分類的 (形容詞)

1186. Mail **delivery** (handing over) was made in spite of the storm.

　註解　遞送 (名詞)

1187. Large **quantities** (amount) of steel are used in automobile production.

　註解　數量 (名詞)

1188. The **index** (indication) shows where each item is located in a book.

　註解　目錄 (名詞)

1189. A **calendar** (kalendar) often gives much more information than just the date.

　註解　日曆 (名詞)

1190. The **production** (creation) of automobiles is the main industry in Michigan.

　註解　產品 (名詞)

1191. The **initial** (first letter) in his name is "S."

　註解　字首 (名詞)

1192. When the colonies received their **independence** (independency) from the British, they had to accept the responsibility of governing their country.

　註解　獨立 (名詞)

1193. Mary had **confidence** (dependence) that Jane could pass her typing exam.

　註解　信任 (名詞)

1194. Because of **gravity** (earth's force) anything which is dropped falls.

　註解　地心吸力 (名詞)

1195. Please **describe** (represent), or tell about, the people who live in that area.

　註解　描述 (動詞)

1196. She weighed 110 pounds on the **scales** (balance).

    註解　天秤 (名詞)

1197. They are going to **surround** (enclose) the house with police protection.

    註解　圍繞 (不定詞)

1198. If you release the air, the balloon will **collapse** (cave in).

    註解　陷縮 (動詞)

1199. The **temperature** (warmth and coldness) was very high today.

    註解　氣溫 (名詞)

1200. The women in the **garment** (clothes) factory made dresses.

    註解　衣服 (名詞)

1201. The dogs were **quarreling** (wrangling) over a bone.

    註解　爭吵 (動詞，進行式)

1202. The store had **merchandise** (commodities) to sell.

    註解　商品 (名詞)

1203. The salesman will receive a **commission** (stipend) for selling the new car.

    註解　酬勞金 (名詞)

1204. The car **cost** (charged) more money than he wanted to spend.

    註解　價值 (動詞)

1205. **Customers** (Patrons) are sometimes hard to please.

    註解　顧客 (名詞)

1206. If one does not pay for furniture, the store will **repossess** (regain possession of) it.

    註解　擁有 (動詞)

1207. John will use his old car as a **down payment** (first pay) on a new one.

    註解　首期款 (名詞片語)

1208. John will **purchase** (procure) a new car next week.

    註解　購買 (動詞)

1209. He wanted to have the **exact** (precise) amount of money for the newsboy.

    註解　正確的 (形容詞)

1210. **Praise** (Laud) for good work is always welcome.

    註解　讚美 (動詞)

1211. It seemed a **miracle** (marvel) that she lived as long as she did with her illness.

    註解　奇怪之事 (名詞)

1212. They found a **site** (location) on which to build their home.

  註解　位置 (名詞)

1213. It was **an adventure** (a peril) for the boys to explore near the river.

  註解　危險 (名詞)

1214. We can see many things through **a microscope** (an optical instrument) that cannot be seen with the naked eye.

  註解　顯微鏡 (名詞)

1215. The highest point of a place is often called a **peak** (pinnacle).

  註解　尖頂 (名詞)

1216. Columbus tried to **discover** (descry) a new route to India.

  註解　發現 (不定詞)

1217. **Fertilizer** (Fertiliser) is used on the fields to produce more corn.

  註解　肥料 (名詞)

1218. Alaska is still considered a **frontier** (boundary) because of its small population in many areas.

  註解　邊界 (名詞)

1219. The city they were passing through was **unfamiliar** (not conversant) to them.

  註解　不熟識的 (名詞)

1220. There was **silence** (stillness) in the school after everyone had gone home.

  註解　安靜 (名詞)

1221. Bill was a **creator** (inventor) of unusual buildings.

  註解　創造者 (名詞)

1222. He will **deliver** (turn over) the furniture to your home.

  註解　交付 (動詞)

1223. The **basement** (underground) usually is cool in the summer.

  註解　地下室 (名詞)

1224. He will **exchange** (commute) this book for another.

  註解　交換 (動詞)

1225. The heart attack was **fatal** (mortal) to the man.

  註解　致命的 (形容詞)

1226. He committed a **felony** (flagrant offence) when robbing the store.

  註解　重罪 (名詞)

1227. There was a great **variety** (assortment) of food on the menu.
   註解 分類 (名詞)

1228. The **address** (lodging) was 120 Grant Street.
   註解 住址 (名詞)

1229. He gave **information** (date) to the police.
   註解 資料，日期 (名詞)

1230. He wrapped books in a **package** (parcel).
   註解 包裹 (名詞)

1231. He gave **first-aid** (emergency succor) to the injured.
   註解 緊急初步的援助 (名詞)

1232. He will **experiment with** (try out) the new machine to make it work properly.
   註解 實驗 (動詞片語)

1233. He was **convicted** (approved) of robbery.
   註解 判有罪 (動詞，被動式)

1234. Because we were near the library every day, we had **access** (approaches) to books.
   註解 研究使用 (名詞)

1235. The **janitor** (superintendent) cleaned the building.
   註解 管理員 (名詞)

1236. Charlie was tipsy in high school, but he is always in **solemn** (august) senses now.
   註解 嚴肅的 (形容詞)

1237. If the will takes the place of the old law, it **supersedes** (replaces) the law.
   註解 替代 (動詞)

1238. A short stay is a **sojourn** (temporary stay).
   註解 逗留 (名詞)

1239. My driver license will **expire** (terminate) in January, 2020.
   註解 到期 (動詞)

1240. Uncle Henry always **shrugs** (raises and contracts) his shoulders and leaves whenever Aunt Jean is angry.
   註解 聳肩 (動詞)

1241. If we drink the tea slowly, we **sip** (absorb) it.
   註解 吸小口 (動詞)

1242. Unless you have a map, our village is very difficult to **locate** (discover).

註解　發現 (不定詞)

1243. Emotional maladjustment is a definite **neurosis** (psychoneurosis).

註解　神經病 (名詞)

1244. Jean stopped her car so **abruptly** (sharply) that she hit the police car.

註解　突然地 (副詞)

1245. The poor woman is **destitute** (indigent) of money.

註解　缺乏的 (形容詞)

1246. You are not supposed to **exploit** (utilize) such a little girl by marking her work for 50 cents an hour.

註解　利用 (不定詞)

1247. Feel sorry for sin and seek forgiveness is to **repent** (regret).

註解　悔悟 (不定詞)

1248. A new electric light is **constructed** (erected).

註解　建立 (動詞，被動式)

1249. Because of inflation, our business is **depressed** (dejected).

註解　蕭條的 (形容詞)

1250. Please do not place too much **emphasis** (stress) on mathematics.

註解　強調 (名詞)

1251. One who is entitled to inherit another's property is an **heir** (inheritor).

註解　繼承人 (名詞)

1252. The traffic court issued a **warrant** (writ) to arrest Mr. Brown for his speeding on Highway 70.

註解　書面命令，拘票 (名詞)

1253. When the little boy lost his toy, his **dejection** (depression) was so great that I, too, became sad.

註解　沮喪 (名詞)

1254. A person who pays rent for the use of land, a building, or a room is a **tenant** (lessee).

註解　承租人 (名詞)

1255. To put off a meeting is to **postpone** (defer) it.

註解　延期 (不定詞)

1256. After criminals are caught, they are **arraigned** (accused) and put on trial.

註解　控告 (動詞，被動式)

1257. If we say the river is sinuous, it is **winding** (sinuous).

> 註解 彎彎曲曲的 (形容詞)

1258. Completely exhausted is **enervated** (languid).

> 註解 衰弱的 (形容詞)

1259. The boss scolded me with **vehemence** (fury).

> 註解 暴怒 (名詞)

1260. I watched a **swarm** (horde) of bees.

> 註解 大群 (名詞)

1261. A group of actors or singers is **rehearsal** (drill).

> 註解 操練 (名詞)

1262. A government official who fills administrative posts with his nephews and his nieces and his cousins by the dozens-quite irrespective of their ability is a **nepotist** (nepotic man).

> 註解 引用親戚 (名詞)

1263. To be more circumspect is to be **cautious** (vigilant).

> 註解 小心的 (形容詞)

1264. Occurring from a feeling of identification with another is **vicarious** (substitute).

> 註解 代替的 (形容詞)

1265. The picture on the wall needs **shifting** (moving).

> 註解 移動 (動名詞)

1266. Because my brother hit me on my face, and I had a serious **bruise** (contusion).

> 註解 瘀傷 (名詞)

1267. Fertile place with water in the desert is **oasis** (fertile area).

> 註解 綠州 (名詞)

1268. How can an old man like me **put up with** (bear) such noise.

> 註解 忍受 (動詞片語)

1269. Those people are paying **homage** (devotion) to the king.

> 註解 效忠，熱愛 (名詞)

1270. If a child were born after the death of his father, he would be **posthumous** (orphan).

> 註解 遺腹子，孤兒 (名詞)

1271. The hospital on Park Avenue has **accommodation** (food and lodging) for fifty patients only.

　　註解　膳宿 (名詞)

1272. The development of a city will always **enhance** (elevate) the land value.

　　註解　增加 (動詞)

1273. To struggle vigorously is to **strive** (toil)

　　註解　努力 (不定詞)

1274. John shouted until he became quite **hoarse** (raucous).

　　註解　沙啞的 (形容詞)

1275. My four-year-old daughter **crouched** (cringed) under the desk, try to hide from my search.

　　註解　蹲躲 (動詞)

1276. An eclipse is an interesting **phenomenon** (prodigy).

　　註解　現象 (名詞)

1277. The baby was **startled** (scared) from sleep.

　　註解　驚嚇 (動詞，被動式)

1278. Not wishing to attend the dance, Marie **feigned** (simulated) illness.

　　註解　假裝 (動詞)

1279. I think Tom and his wife **insult** (offend) me so much that I begin to hate them.

　　註解　侮辱 (動詞)

1280. The little girl has the strong **resemblance** (analogy) to his father.

　　註解　相似 (名詞)

1281. This animal has now become **extinct** (vanished).

　　註解　滅種的 (形容詞)

1282. A shallow place in a river that can be crossed by walking or in an automobile is **ford** (bank).

　　註解　淺灘 (名詞)

1283. If you keep bread too long, it becomes **stale** (insipid).

　　註解　不新鮮的，沒味道的 (形容詞)

1284. John earns extra money every summer by picking apples in one of his uncle's **orchards** (fruit gardens).

　　註解　果園 (名詞)

1285. The orange is full of vitality, and it is **juicy** (succulent).

　　　註解　　多汁的 (形容詞)

1286. The robbers got the money out of their **plunder** (loot).

　　　註解　　贓物 (名詞)

1287. When I reached the station, the train was leaving as **scheduled** (tabled).

　　　註解　　時程的 (形容詞)

1288. If a man takes action before he thinks, he is **impetuous** (impulsive).

　　　註解　　衝動的 (形容詞)

1289. To make love triflingly is to **philander** (dally).

　　　註解　　調戲 (不定詞)

1290. A naive attitude is **unsophisticated** (ingenuous).

　　　註解　　天眞的 (形容詞)

1291. To pull with force and transport by wagon is to **haul** (drag).

　　　註解　　拖拉 (不定詞)

1292. The sale is **transacted** (enacted) in the lawyer's office.

　　　註解　　處理 (動詞，被動式)

1293. They were held as **hostages** (pledges) by the enemy.

　　　註解　　人質 (名詞)

1294. Because I am broke, I wish to ask you for a **loan** (lending).

　　　註解　　借貸 (名詞)

1295. It **stands** (symbolizes) for the unknown quantity.

　　　註解　　表示 (動詞)

1296. Sheer and gauzy material is **diaphanous** (transparent).

　　　註解　　透明的 (形容詞)

1297. Since he owes me a lot of money, I'll have to **sue** (charge) him in the court.

　　　註解　　控告 (不定詞)

1298. A medal was **awarded** (bestowed) to him for his past services.

　　　註解　　獎賞 (動詞 被動式)

1299. He questions everything, even the existence of God. He's a **skeptic** (atheist).

　　　註解　　懷疑論者，無神論者 (名詞)

1300. It is unfair, and I was **reluctant** (loath) to pay the electricity bill.

　　　註解　　不願意的 (形容詞)

1301. A tyro is a **beginner** (novice).

　　　註解　新手 (名詞)

1302. To be genial and merry is said to be **jovial** (mirthful).

　　　註解　快樂的 (形容詞)

1303. The mother of children would **discard** (dismiss) the old toys and buy new ones.

　　　註解　拋棄 (動詞)

1304. To struggle awkwardly to move is to **flounder** (withstand).

　　　註解　掙扎 (不定詞)

1305. One who believes that there is no God but the combined forces and laws which are manifested in the existing universe is a **pantheist** (pantheistic man).

　　　註解　多神論者 (名詞)

1306. Since this business is not making any money, I am very **indifferent** (apathetic) to it.

　　　註解　不關心的 (形容詞)

1307. To send a messenger is to **dispatch** (send off).

　　　註解　派遣 (不定詞)

1308. To vacillate continuously is to **waver** (flutter) mentally.

　　　註解　搖擺 (不定詞)

1309. The woman was trying to make the fruit cakes, but she was without **ingredients** (constituents).

　　　註解　成份，要素 (名詞)

1310. When Martha dropped the plate, it **shattered** (shivered).

　　　註解　粉碎 (動詞)

1311. The baby cried loudly and **spilt** (dispersed) the milk all over the rug.

　　　註解　吐出 (動詞)

1312. A noisy fight or quarrel is a **brawl** (tumult).

　　　註解　爭吵 (名詞)

1313. An **egregious** (glaring) blunder is outstandingly bad.

　　　註解　過份的 (形容詞)

1314. The evenings here are too cool to be comfortable; they are really quite **chilly** (frigid).

　　　註解　酷寒的 (形容詞)

1315. You may go out if there is a **lull** (tranquility) in the storm.

註解 平靜 (名詞)

1316. To be sorry about is to **deplore** (lament).

註解 深悔，悲傷 (不定詞)

1317. Mayor Jones is popular in Spring Field, California and he is **confident** (positive) that he can be elected again.

註解 確信的 (形容詞)

1318. The Graduating Class had to **disband** (dissolve) its music club.

註解 解散 (不定詞)

1319. To give a suggestion is to **hint** (imply).

註解 暗示 (不定詞)

1320. There must be something wrong with Bob's leg for he is **limping** (laming) badly.

註解 跛行的 (形容詞)

1321. The general **disposed** (regulated) his troops very well.

註解 佈署 (動詞)

1322. The dog must have been **stray** (wandering) for he hasn't come home for a week.

註解 迷路的 (形容詞)

1323. The officers are still meeting, but they plan to **adjourn** (suspend) very soon.

註解 休會，暫停 (不定詞)

1324. Mrs. Fred was very sad, but her sad feeling was **transitory** (impermanent).

註解 暫時的 (形容詞)

1325. Mrs. Morre was very angry and **violently** (immoderately) walked over those broken glasses.

註解 激烈地 (副詞)

1326. The **fine** (mulct) for littering the highway is at least twenty-five dollars in Illinois.

註解 罰金 (名詞)

1327. The dog was taught to **retake** (recapture) the ball that had been thrown away.

註解 取回 (不定詞)

1328. The man was afraid to eat the apple because it looked **rotten** (putrid).

   註解　腐爛的 (形容詞)

1329. Excessively positive in manner or utterance is **dogmatic** (opinionated).

   註解　武斷的 (形容詞)

1330. He **snored** (breathed harshly) while he was sleeping.

   註解　打鼾 (動詞)

1331. A new electric light is **installed** (placed)

   註解　安裝 (動詞，被動式)

1332. A problem or a puzzle in the form of a question is called a **riddle** (conundrum).

   註解　謎題 (名詞)

1333. The Olympic Games **drew to an end** (ceased).

   註解　結束 (動詞片語)

1334. When he was banished from his country, he lived in **exile** (expatriation).

   註解　放逐 (名詞)

1335. If it is warm and comfortable, it is **cosy** (snug).

   註解　舒適的 (形容詞，同 cozy)

1336. Mrs. Jones sat by the window **mending** (restoring) the hole in her coat.

   註解　修補 (動名詞)

1337. Spiteful hatred is **rancor** (venom).

   註解　怨恨 (名詞)

1338. Young girl should know how to **get along** (manage) by themselves.

   註解　支配，過活 (不定詞片語)

1339. We must save money **toward** (for) the children's education.

   註解　為了 (介系詞)

1340. An enemy is your **foe** (antagonist).

   註解　敵人 (名詞)

1341. We know there must be a fire because we can see the **sparks** (fiery particles).

   註解　火花 (名詞)

1342. To beg or ask people sincerely is to **beseech** (solicit).

   註解　懇求 (不定詞)

1343. He is too **ingenuous** (artless) to try to deceive you.

   註解　老實的 (形容詞)

1344. The girl had quiet, modest **demeanor** (deportment).

> 註解 舉動 (名詞)

1345. If the temperature were much lower, Anna's coat would be too **light** (thin) to keep her warm.

> 註解 單薄的 (形容詞)

1346. The teacher **chide** (nagged) me for my fault.

> 註解 責備 (動詞)

1347. If the rain did not stop all night, the rain did not **let up** (stop).

> 註解 停止 (動詞片語)

1348. To consider carefully is to **ponder** (deliberate).

> 註解 深思 (不定詞)

1349. When he forced himself to come in without invitation, he **intruded** (interloped).

> 註解 闖入 (動詞)

1350. **At times** (Occasionally) he prepares his lessons well, at other times he does very poor work.

> 註解 偶爾地 (副詞)

1351. I **ran into** (met accidentally) Joe, who was on his way to the hotel to see how I was getting along.

> 註解 偶然相遇 (動詞片語)

1352. You must carry them very carefully, because they are **fragile** (delicate).

> 註解 易破碎的 (形容詞)

1353. To make or to become smaller is to **dwindle** (wane).

> 註解 縮小 (不定詞)

1354. They **tore away** (demolished) the old building.

> 註解 拆毀 (動詞片語)

1355. He spent all his money through **extravagance** (profusion).

> 註解 浪費 (名詞)

1356. A song for lulling a baby to sleep is a **lullaby** (cradlesong)

> 註解 搖籃曲 (名詞)

1357. Mary's parents went to a dance school and found the music **detestable** (abominable) then complained and left.

> 註解 可惡的 (形容詞)

1358. Mary wanted to go to the dance with Dave but Dave was always busy. Mary was **disgusted** (nauseated).

> 註解 厭惡的 (形容詞)

1359. We'll **think over** (muse upon) your offer and give you our answer in the morning.

> 註解 考慮 (動詞片語)

1360. The twenty-six states that do **observe** (maintain) the holiday celebrate it either on February 12 or the first Monday in Feb.

> 註解 維持 (動詞)

1361. If you want to look up the meaning of a word you consult a **lexicon** (dictionary).

> 註解 字典 (名詞)

1362. If he is an **indefatigable** (unfatigued) person, he will be tireless.

> 註解 不疲倦的 (形容詞)

1363. The train wreck in which fifty people were killed was a **disaster** (misfortune).

> 註解 災難 (名詞)

1364. The order to stay in one's own bailiwick means that a person should remain in his own **district** (locality).

> 註解 立場 (名詞)

1365. He finished his piano recital with great éclat. His performance was **brilliant** (lustrous).

> 註解 亮麗的 (形容詞)

1366. When the old woman was needling, she was so careless that she unfortunately **pricked** (punctured) her own hand.

> 註解 刺到 (動詞)

1367. My problem of what courses to take is **perplexing** (confounding).

> 註解 困惑的 (形容詞)

1368. A disease due to lack of fresh fruit and vegetables is **scurvy** (bleeding illness).

> 註解 壞血症 (名詞)

1369. Because I can see the mountain, it is **conspicuous** (salient).

> 註解 明顯的 (形容詞

1370. We don't like John because he has a habit of **meddling** (officious).

　　　註解　干擾的 (動名詞，同義字爲形容詞)

1371. He is **resolute** (steadfast) in doing his assignments.

　　　註解　堅決的 (形容詞)

1372. Mrs. Jones **beckoned** (gestured) them to come nearer.

　　　註解　招手 (動詞)

1373. There are many trees thickly covered with **foliage** (leafage).

　　　註解　樹葉 (名詞)

1374. If Professor Baker is extremely eager, he is **keen** (fervid).

　　　註解　熱心的 (形容詞)

1375. The woman always use baby talk to **cajole** (wheedle) favors from the trusting male.

　　　註解　甜言蜜語 (不定詞)

1376. It is unfortunate that you are always making **implications** (involvements) about your friends dishonesty.

　　　註解　暗示 (名詞)

1377. The **repercussion** (echo) of an event must happen after.

　　　註解　反應，回聲 (名詞)

1378. To make a short journey for pleasure is a **jaunt** (excursion).

　　　註解　遠足 (名詞)

1379. The thief agreed to make restitution for his **defalcation** (misappropriation).

　　　註解　盜用公款 (名詞)

1380. This white horse is **docile** (tractable).

　　　註解　過順的 (形容詞)

1381. If he is evil and shabby, he is **sinister** (wicked).

　　　註解　陰陰的 (形容詞)

1382. **Cursory** (Superficial) reading is very fast.

　　　註解　粗略的 (形容詞)

1383. A vindictive person is one who is **revengeful** (malevolent).

　　　註解　惡意的 (形容詞)

1384. Mary is leaving her job **for good** (forever).

　　　註解　永久地 (副詞)

1385. Henry is **supposed** to (is assumed to) be at work at 8 o'clock, but he arrived at 9 this morning.

　　註解　應該 (動詞，要用被動式)

1386. We won three times, lost five times, and **tied** (made the same score) twice.

　　註解　平手 (動詞)

1387. It leaves at 3:50, but you must check in one hour **prior** (anterior) to departure.

　　註解　以前的 (形容詞)

1388. Peter and Lucy had a quarrel, but they soon **made up** (reconciled).

　　註解　和好 (動詞片語)

1389. I couldn't because my political science lecture **let out** (ended) too late.

　　註解　結束 (動詞片語)

1390. What is the one **drawback** (hindrance) of the new store according to the woman?

　　註解　障礙 (名詞)

1391. I've got to write a long composition for my English class, and I just can't **come up with** (approach) any ideas, and it's due tomorrow.

　　註解　達到，追上 (動詞片語)

1392. I've been trying to finish this research project for that I can present my findings at the **annual** (yearly) conference in July.

　　註解　年度的 (形容詞)

1393. In 1927 Borghum began this **monumental** (massive) task when he was sixty years old.

　　註解　巨大的 (形容詞)

1394. Upon John's death, his son continued the project until the funding **ran out** (used up).

　　註解　用完 (動詞片語)

1395. I promised to **babysit** (take charge of children) for my neighbors while they go to a military dinner.

　　註解　當褓姆 (不定詞)

1396. The man were rescued after waving **frantically** (frenziedly) at a private airplane flying overhead.

　　註解　瘋狂地 (副詞)

1397. He was **recuperating** (healing) in the hospital while his bones were mending, most of which were broken.

| 註解 | 休養，治療 (動詞，進行式)

1398. The aluminum satellite is not expect to **disintegrate** (break up) on reentry.

| 註解 | 分裂 (不定詞)

1399. Lucy couldn't wear the wool coat because it made her **break out** (arise) in a rash.

| 註解 | 發生 (動詞，使役動詞之後用原型動詞)

1400. **Despite** (Notwithstanding) his inexperience in the field, Phil applied for the job.

| 註解 | 不管 (介系詞)

1401. The response to our initial request was **gratifying** (satisfying).

| 註解 | 令人滿意的 (形容詞)

1402. She **ran out of** (exhausted) milk and went out to get some.

| 註解 | 用完 (動詞片語)

1403. She **came down with** (became affected with) the flu and had to stay home.

| 註解 | 遭受 (動詞片語)

1404. We had to **cross off** (revoke) fifteen names from our original list of one hundred.

| 註解 | 消除 (不定詞片語)

1405. He's got so many bills that his wife says that he will never **get ahead** (be successful).

| 註解 | 成功 (動詞片語)

1406. Not getting that job was a big **letdown** (disappointment).

| 註解 | 失望 (名詞)

1407. Maria's eyes are **irritated** (inflamed) from the chlorine in the pool.

| 註解 | 發炎紅腫的 (形容詞)

1408. The play certainly raised some eyebrows, but it was nothing less than **hilarious** (cheerful).

| 註解 | 高興的 (形容詞)

1409. Chuck said that they got a very good **deal** (bargain) on it.

| 註解 | 廉價 (名詞)

1410. The program director said that we'd have to postpone the outing until Saturday because of **inclement** (harsh) weather.

   註解　嚴寒的 (形容詞)

1411. It's not as direct as the bus, but it's faster and there will be less chance of a **traffic jam** (vehicle crowd).

   註解　交通阻塞 (名詞片語)

1412. A short time later, he awoke; his legs were **numb** (feelingless) and he was trembling.

   註解　麻木的 (形容詞)

1413. Edwas lost his sight as a result of **trauma** (body injury) in a terrible accident.

   註解　創傷 (名詞)

1414. In colonial days, Delaware was part of the "bread basket" area, raising wheat, corn, and other grains for national **consumption** (expenditure).

   註解　消耗 (名詞)

1415. The one with the green sweater using the **crutches** (staffs).

   註解　拐杖 (名詞)

1416. Did you hear that the neighborhood convenience store was **held up** (robbed) last night?

   註解　搶劫 (動詞片語，被動式)

1417. I think your red dress would be more **elegant** (luxurious) for the reception.

   註解　高雅的 (形容詞)

1418. **Adaptation** (Conformation) is the process by which living things adjust to changes in their environment.

   註解　適應 (名詞)

1419. There brave adventures depended solely on the wind **velocity** (swiftness).

   註解　速度 (名詞)

1420. All living, self-propelled beings do not enjoy the same **lifespan** (longevity).

   註解　壽命 (名詞)

1421. Some animals are **carnivorous** (flesh-eating) but some others are herbivorous.

   註解　肉食的 (形容詞)

1422. With all the **overtime** (extra pay) he had last week, Ron should be able to buy the new coat he's been wanting.

　註解　超時 (名詞)

1423. I'd really like to get your **recipe** (instruction) for that chocolate cake you made tonight.

　註解　食譜 (名詞)

1424. You know that everyone is eligible for the draft, and I don't think your old football injury is going to **exempt** (release) you.

　註解　免除 (不定詞)

1425. He put a wreath of flowers in the vase and **comforted** (solaced) him.

　註解　安慰 (動詞)

1426. His aunt was very sick, and she **passed away** (died) last summer.

　註解　逝世 (動詞片語)

1427. You just take it easy, and then you will **pull through** (survive).

　註解　渡過難關 (動詞片語)

1428. John **substituted** (replaced) chemistry for biology in the last fall semester.

　註解　以…代替 (動詞)

1429. Flying is **appreciably** (considerably) faster than driving, so if Bill sets out from Chicago to Los Angeles in an airplane and Jim does the same in a car.

　註解　可估計地 (副詞)

1430. I can't stand that kind of music. It's so **superficial** (shallow).

　註解　膚淺的 (形容詞)

1431. Can you give me a hand? This box is very **bulky** (cumbersome).

　註解　笨重的 (形容詞)

1432. I think that the weather is not so **unfavorable** (adverse) that it can't arrive.

　註解　不利的 (形容詞)

1433. Mario is an expert in tennis and skiing, but he never **mastered** (subdued) swimming.

　註解　克服 (動詞)

1434. The **issue** (problem) of women's rights has part of the American scene since the last century.
> 註解　問題 (名詞)

1435. If Alice were **single** (unwed), she would travel.
> 註解　未婚的 (形容詞)

1436. I adore chamber music, but I have no **patience** (forbearance) with the 20th century stuff, especially that awful electronic noise.
> 註解　忍受 (名詞)

1437. Sally left at 8:00, and Julie, late as usual, **dashed out** (went out) 20 minutes later.
> 註解　匆促外出 (動詞片語)

1438. I **banged** (slammed) my arm against the corner of the coffee table while I was playing with my son.
> 註解　撞擊 (動詞)

1439. Sometimes it is difficult to understand why we must **endure** (tolerate) painful disappointment.
> 註解　忍耐 (動詞)

1440. Jim and Barbara could not agree on what movie they wanted to see, so they decided to **flip** (toss) a coin.
> 註解　投擲 (不定詞)

1441. Alice was almost **decapitated** (beheaded) during the school play.
> 註解　砍頭 (動詞，被動式)

1442. **Customarily** (Habitually), our clothing is solemn for funerals and gay for weddings.
> 註解　習俗地 (副詞)

1443. She has felt **lonely** (solitary) ever since her brother left for Japan.
> 註解　孤獨的 (形容詞)

1444. Don't tell him about it. He'll become **furious** (raged).
> 註解　發怒地 (形容詞)

1445. We'll keep the windows open while we **inspect** (scrutinize) it.
> 註解　細查 (動詞)

1446. I don't mind **suspense** (incertitude), but I really don't see the need to show all the blood and guts.
> 註解　不確定 (名詞)

1447. **Unwittingly** (Unconsciously) the teacher gave away the answer to the question.

   註解　不經意地 (副詞)

1448. The plainsmen of Australia are often annoyed by **dingoes** (wild dogs).

   註解　野狗 (名詞)

1449. The angry mob **liberated** (set free) the prisoners.

   註解　釋放 (動詞)

1450. Robin Hood's men were brought to trial for **poaching** (taking game or fish by illegal methods) in the king's forests.

   註解　不法狩獵 (動名詞)

1451. Kangaroos and opossums are both **marsupial** (animals carrying young in pouches).

   註解　有袋的動物 (名詞)

1452. Through irrigation **arid** (dry) sections of the country have been made productive.

   註解　乾燥的 (形容詞)

1453. The artist was noted for his paintings of **pastoral** (rural) scenes.

   註解　田園的 (形容詞)

1454. The hurricane caused **irreparable** (unable to be repaired) damage.

   註解　不能挽回的 (形容詞)

1455. What the man politely said to the policeman was not indicating (giving sign or suggestion) of wat he really felt.

   註解　暗示 (動詞，進行式)

1456. **Psychopathic** (Pertaining to mental disorders) patients are confined to one ward in the hospital.

   註解　精神病的 (形容詞)

1457. By **eradicating** (destroying completely) slum areas, the city may control delinquency.

   註解　根除 (動名詞)

1458. The **ironical** (contrary to the expected, satirical) feature of the situation is that the home team has never won a homecoming game on this field.

   註解　諷刺的 (形容詞)

1459. On the highway speeders are a **menace** (that which threatens to cause evil or harm).

    註解　威嚇 (名詞)

1460. The **computation** (act of figuring up, estimating) of the interest took the bank clerk considerable time.

    註解　計算 (名詞)

1461. The **husky** (Eskimo dog) dragged the sled across the frozen lake.

    註解　愛斯基摩狗 (名詞)

1462. **Warily** (Cautiously), the old man crossed the crowded street.

    註解　小心地 (副詞)

1463. The tight rope walker **momentarily** (for an instant) lost his balance.

    註解　時時刻刻地 (副詞)

1464. **Incredulously** (Unbelievingly), the winner looked at the prize money.

    註解　不能相信地 (副詞)

1465. The wind howled **ominously** (in a threatening manner).

    註解　有惡兆地 (副詞)

1466. As the season progressed, the popularity of the football player **waned** (decreased).

    註解　無力，減少 (動詞)

1467. During the flood the children were **marooned** (left helpless and alone) in the old schoolhouse.

    註解　孤獨無助的 (形容詞)

1468. The aviator had no **alternative** (chance to choose course of action) but to parachute to safety.

    註解　選擇 (名詞)

1469. Her husband's death left a **void** (feeling of emptiness) in her life she knew would never be filled.

    註解　空虛 (名詞)

1470. His parents hope that **ultimately** (finally) he will become a doctor.

    註解　最後地 (副詞)

1471. The candidate **committed** (pledged) himself to many promises he could not keep.

    註解　保證 (動詞)

1472. His own bad temper was his **arch-enemy** (chief-enemy).
　　註解　主要的敵人 (名詞)

1473. Supply usually influences the value of a(n) **commodity** (article of trade).
　　註解　商品 (名詞)

1474. When the teacher left the room, complete **chaos** (confusion) ruled.
　　註解　混亂 (名詞)

1475. Arrange the topics in a **logical** (reasonable) order so that reader will understand.
　　註解　條理的 (形容詞)

1476. Because the college boys had little money, they decided to travel in **steerage** (part of ship with cheapest traveling rates) to Europe.
　　註解　客船之統艙 (名詞)

1477. The girl **resolved** (determined) to have her assignments on time.
　　註解　決定 (動詞)

1478. The power of the wheel came from a **treadmill** (mill kept in motion by an animal or person walking on a wheel or belt).
　　註解　獸力或人力旋轉車 (名詞)

1479. They cut **cordwood** (wood cut and stocked to measurement) with a power saw.
　　註解　堆積之木材 (名詞)

1480. She **takes a dim view of** (lacks enthusiasm for) games.
　　註解　不感興趣 (動詞片語)

1481. The supply of water is **vital** (of extreme importance).
　　註解　重要的 (形容詞)

1482. The family traveled by **Conestoga wagon** (large covered wagon).
　　註解　四輪馬車 (名詞)

1483. The firm was declared **bankrupt** (unable to pay debts).
　　註解　破產的 (形容詞)

1484. We were afraid of a **concussion** (shaking or shocking).
　　註解　震動 (名詞)

1485. The **turnpike** (road having toll gates) was constructed with shoulders.
　　註解　收費關卡 (名詞)

1486. The sound came at **intervals** (particular times or places).
　　註解　間隔時間 (名詞)

1487. The **meteorite** (iron mass from outer space) fell on the western plains.

   | 註解 | 逆向的 (形容詞)

1488. The **meteorite** (iron mass from outer space) fell on the western plains.

   | 註解 | 隕石 (名詞)

1489. Numerous ditches and gullies caused by **erosion** (wearing away by water) reduced the value of the farm.

   | 註解 | 沖蝕 (名詞)

1490. **Majestically** (In a proud, dignified manner), the big ship into the harbor, every sail gleaming in the sunlight.

   | 註解 | 宏大地 (副詞)

1491. The senior class activities **culminated** (reached highest point) in the commencement exercises and graduation dance.

   | 註解 | 達於頂點 (動詞)

1492. The old man was **partially** (not completely) blind.

   | 註解 | 部份地 (副詞)

1493. The witness **confirmed** (declared to be true) the statement made by the prisoner.

   | 註解 | 證實 (動詞)

1494. The priests made a **pilgrimage** (journey) to the holy city.

   | 註解 | 朝聖之旅 (名詞)

1495. The woodsman **lashed** (tied) the logs with a rope before setting them afloat.

   | 註解 | 綑緊 (動詞)

1496. The **assay** (determining weight and quality) office sent the report on the ore to the mining company.

   | 註解 | 試驗所 (名詞)

1497. The medicine had a **metallic** (resembling metal) taste.

   | 註解 | 金屬的 (形容詞)

1498. All members must learn the **ritual** (code of ceremonies) of the lodge when they are initiated.

   | 註解 | 儀式 (名詞)

1499. From the top of the **knoll** (small hill) we had a view of the valley.

   | 註解 | 小山丘 (名詞)

1500. The **massive** (huge) statue was larger than any of the surrounding sculpture.

   註解　巨大的 (形容詞)

1501. **Yaupons** (kind of hollies) grow in the warm climates.

   註解　冬青樹 (名詞)

1502. The house was made of **buff-colored** (medium tan) bricks.

   註解　淺黃色的 (形容詞)

1503. The fishermen sat on the pier mending their **seines** (nets).

   註解　捕魚網 (名詞)

1504. The child was delighted with the **miniature** (small) furniture for the doll house.

   註解　小小的 (形容詞)

1505. **Blennies** (Kind of fish) usually are found in salt water rather than fresh water.

   註解　黏魚(名詞)

1506. We tried **luring** (tempting) the birds to our yard with crumbs and seeds.

   註解　引誘 (動名詞)

1507. The fire cast **spectral** (ghost-like) shadows against the wall.

   註解　妖怪的 (形容詞)

1508. The orchestra played a **medley** (mixture) of tunes from the operettas of Gilbert and Sullivan.

   註解　混合曲 (名詞)

1509. The prisoners tried to **appease** (calm, satisfy) the native chief with gifts of beads and colored ribbon.

   註解　緩和 (不定詞)

1510. Many **crustaceans** (fish having a shell-like covering) are good to eat.

   註解　甲殼類動物 (名詞)

1511. Bob's **placid** (calm) disposition annoyed his energetic older brother.

   註解　安靜的 (形容詞)

1512. **Winnowing** (Flapping) wings disturbed the stillness of the air.

   註解　吹散的 (形容詞)

1513. The **ebbing** (receding, flowing back) waters left seaweed and shells scattered along the beach.

   註解　退潮的 (形容詞)

1514. The **silhouette** (outline) of the lone tree against the gray sky created a mournful picture.

    註解　影像 (名詞)

1515. In his views of the society he is a **dissenter** (one who disagrees).

    註解　異議份子 (名詞)

1516. For defense they had a **howitzer** (kind of cannon).

    註解　榴彈砲 (名詞)

1517. The man will try to **retaliate** (pay back).

    註解　歸還 (不定詞)

1518. His father **vouchsafed** (acknowledged) that it was true.

    註解　回音，認知 (動詞)

1519. He will **perpetrate** (commit) a deed of violence.

    註解　觸犯 (動詞)

1520. The instructor used **ingenuity** (cleverness).

    註解　智慧 (名詞)

1521. The **depredations** (robberies) of bandits became a major concern.

    註解　搶奪 (名詞)

1522. The **garrison** (soldiers in a fort) was dismissed ceremoniously.

    註解　衛戍部隊 (名詞)

1523. The **watershed** (ridge dividing drainage area) has been thoroughly explored.

    註解　分水嶺 (名詞)

1524. The act was really **sadism** (love of cruelty).

    註解　虐待狂 (名詞)

1525. Charles is a **nominal** (in name) believer.

    註解　名義上的 (形容詞)

1526. The people were not **paragon** (models of excellence).

    註解　模範 (名詞)

1527. His **infamy** (wickedness) will live in history.

    註解　醜名 (名詞)

1528. He proved to be a faithful **henchman** (follower).

    註解　親信 (名詞)

1529. The species is threatened with **extinction** (wiping out completely).

    註解　毀滅 (名詞)

1530. Many people claim they suffer from **insomnia** (sleeplessness) when really sleep very well.

　　　註解　失眠症 (名詞)

1531. The bank failed because its president **adamantly** (stubbornly) refused to change his policies.

　　　註解　堅定地 (副詞)

1532. A pupil may enter one piece of writing in each of the four **categories** (divisions) in the literary contest.

　　　註解　分類 (名詞)

1533. Doctors often prescribe **sedatives** (that which soothes or calms) for their patients who suffer nerve disorders.

　　　註解　鎮定劑 (名詞)

1534. The meeting revealed **diverse** (different) opinions on the subject.

　　　註解　不同的 (形容詞)

1535. That the pupil has studied is **evidenced** (made clear) by his improved grades.

　　　註解　證明 (動詞，被動式)

1536. She **reproached** (found fault with) her friend for being late.

　　　註解　責備 (動詞)

1537. Most people dislike **tepid** (slightly warm) coffee.

　　　註解　微溫的 (形容詞)

1538. **Marinated** (Soaked, as in oil and vinegar) herring is a delicious appetizer.

　　　註解　浸調味料的 (形容詞)

1539. The affairs of the businessman had reached a **crisis** (turning point, dangerous point), and he could no longer avoid a decision.

　　　註解　危機 (名詞)

1540. The **alleged** (declared or claimed to be) thief was proved innocent.

　　　註解　宣稱的 (形容詞)

1541. Reading detective stories is a popular form of **escapism** (relief from routine or reality).

　　　註解　逃避現實 (名詞)

1542. Because of a **depleted** (exhausted) oil supply, the country had to surrender.

　　　註解　耗盡的 (形容詞)

1543. Many people did not approve the **tactics** (methods or schemes) of the wealthy business man.

註解 策略 (名詞)

1544. The **depredations** (acts of raiding and plundering) of the Indians on the settlements brought the army to the territory.

註解 蹂躪 (名詞)

1545. To **evade** (avoid) questioning, the boy slipped out the back door.

註解 逃避 (不定詞)

1546. **Yearling** (one year old) beef is cheaper than some other grades.

註解 一歲的 (形容詞)

1547. Workmen usually **succumb** (yield) to the temptation of higher wages.

註解 屈服 (動詞)

1548. The knight easily defeated his **adversary** (opponent) in the tournament.

註解 敵對手 (名詞)

1549. The natives **revered** (admired and honored) some animals as gods.

註解 崇拜 (動詞)

1550. The book contained **anecdotes** (incidents) of many famous men.

註解 軼事，趣聞 (名詞)

1551. The inventor was **actuated** (aroused to action) by a desire to help his fellow men.

註解 刺激 (動詞，被動式)

1552. A border of **perennial** (living from year to year) flowers surrounded the pool.

註解 四季不斷的 (形容詞)

1553. Disease rather than the enemy **vanquished** (conquered) the army.

註解 征服 (動詞)

1554. A child frequently makes a **sagacious** (shrewd, wise) remark without knowing it.

註解 聰明的 (形容詞)

1555. The landlord chose the furniture for its **utilitarian** (useful) value rather than its beauty.

註解 實用性 (名詞)

1556. We found the trunk in an **obscure** (dark) corner of the attic.

註解 陰暗的 (形容詞)

1557. The **peons** (laborers) earned only a few cents a day working in the fields.

　　註解　工人 (名詞)

1558. I **judiciously** (wisely) left the room when the argument began.

　　註解　明智地 (副詞)

1559. The army outpost occupied a **vulnerable** (capable of being attached) position.

　　註解　易受攻擊的 (形容詞)

1560. Near the kennel the farmer found three **whelps** (puppies), shivering and whining.

　　註解　幼犬 (名詞)

1561. Grandfather was a true **epicure** (judge of good food) and always took us to the best restaurants.

　　註解　美食美酒主義者 (名詞)

1562. His skill is **attested** (proved) by the fact that he assembled the parts in less than five minutes.

　　註解　證實 (動詞，被動式)

1563. The lady, although old, was still **fastidious** (extremely careful and refined) about her dress.

　　註解　吹毛求疵的 (形容詞)

1564. **Extermination** (Complete destruction) of all insects is not desirable.

　　註解　消滅 (名詞)

1565. The experienced hunter knew exactly how to **hamstring** (disable) the beast.

　　註解　使殘廢 (不定詞)

1566. For a young person Mary wore extremely **drab** (dull) clothing.

　　註解　單調的 (形容詞)

1567. Mother repeated her **admonition** (warning) that we be home early.

　　註解　警告 (名詞)

1568. The **hostile** (unfriendly) attitude of the young boy irritated the judge.

　　註解　不友善的 (形容詞)

1569. Sunlight **filtered** (passed slowly or lightly) through the heavy clouds.

　　註解　滲透 (動詞)

1570. To cross the river the soldiers constructed a **pontoon** (floating structure) bridge.

> 註解　浮橋 (名詞)

1571. Because of modern **technology** (industrial science) many jobs in factories have been eliminated.

> 註解　工藝學 (名詞)

1572. The **symmetrical** (balanced) arrangement of the flowers made the decorations appear stiff and formal.

> 註解　對稱的 (形容詞)

1573. During the snow storm the **musher** (sled driver) and his dog plunged through the ice.

> 註解　雪橇夫 (名詞)

1574. The mayor has no **jurisdiction** (authority, control) over county affairs.

> 註解　管控 (名詞)

1575. The officers appeared in **mufti** (civilian dress) at the party.

> 註解　便服 (名詞)

1576. In his travels the salesman from New York was surprised at some of the **provincial** (local) customs and foods.

> 註解　地方的 (形容詞)

1577. The teacher kept the **unruly** (stubborn and disobedient) pupils after school.

> 註解　不守法的 (形容詞)

1578. Some of the **doggerel** (light, humorous verse) in Look Magazine is extremely amusing.

> 註解　詩句 (名詞)

1579. The Curies did much scientific experimentation with **pitchblende** (mineral).

> 註解　瀝青鈾礦 (名詞)

1580. Geometry has **superseded** (replaced) algebra as his favorite subject.

> 註解　替代 (動詞，完成式)

1581. Some girls make a **fetish** (object of special devotion) of clothes.

> 註解　偶像 (名詞)

1582. The mother with her two **moppets** (small children) presented an attractive picture.

　　　註解　小孩 (名詞)

1583. By **synchronizing** (causing to happen at the same time) the attack of the army and navy forces, the commander achieved victory.

　　　註解　同時發生 (動名詞)

1584. The new machine does not **function** (work) properly.

　　　註解　功效，運作 (動詞)

1585. The sales department works in close **liaison** (communication) with the engineering department.

　　　註解　聯絡 (名詞)

1586. The **wrangler** (herder) galloped across the plain, singing to himself.

　　　註解　放牧人 (名詞)

1587. During the gold rush any kind of housing was at a **premium** (high or extra value).

　　　註解　格外價格 (名詞)

1588. One division of the police department deals with **ballistics** (study of firearms).

　　　註解　彈道學 (名詞)

1589. The victory of the army was due largely to the tireless escort work of the **corvettes** (gunboats).

　　　註解　小軍艦 (名詞)

1590. Benjamin Franklin is responsible for many a **maxim** (short rule of conduct) quoted today.

　　　註解　格言 (名詞)

1591. The **marauders** (raiders) ransacked every home in the village.

　　　註解　盜匪 (名詞)

1592. The characters the author describes are entirely **fictional** (imaginary).

　　　註解　虛構的 (形容詞)

1593. When the dictator was at the **zenith** (highest point) of his power, he controlled all the offices of government.

　　　註解　頂點 (名詞)

1594. The old man showed amazing **exuberance** (liveliness).

    註解 豐富，生動 (名詞，同 exuberancy)

1595. The **porcine** (pig-like) beauty amazed us.

    註解 像豬的 (形容詞)

1596. From a distance it appeared to be **bravado** (false courage).

    註解 逞強 (名詞)

1597. All the women spoke **judicially** (in a fair manner).

    註解 公正地 (副詞)

1598. It was difficult to **warrant** (justify) his abuse.

    註解 判斷 (不定詞)

1599. The **consternation** (dismay) was breath-taking.

    註解 恐怖 (名詞)

1600. The duke spoke **sententiously** (tersely).

    註解 簡潔地 (副詞)

1601. The crow called **lustily** (vigorously) from the tree.

    註解 快活地 (副詞)

1602. The uncle was **ostentatious** (showed unnecessary display).

    註解 誇張的 (形容詞)

1603. They bought some **succulent** (juicy) vegetables.

    註解 多汁的 (形容詞)

1604. We became interested in its **rotundity** (plumpness).

    註解 肥胖 (名詞)

1605. The man spoke **succinctly** (concisely).

    註解 簡明地 (副詞)

1606. **Awed** (Inspired with solemn wonder) tourists gaze into the Grand Canyon.

    註解 敬畏的 (形容詞)

1607. **Gauzy** (Very thin and transparent) draperies fluttered in the breeze.

    註解 如紗透明的 (形容詞)

1608. The **scarab** (large, black beetle held in regard by Egyptians) pin contained costly jewels.

    註解 古埃及雕像 (名詞)

1609. The wire must be strong but **pliable** (easily bent).

    註解 易彎曲的 (形容詞)

1610. We were afraid to sit on the **insubstantial** (flimsy, not solid or strong) looking chairs.

   註解　薄弱的 (形容詞)

1611. Most hospitals have **auxiliary** (furnishing) power plants for use in case of emergency.

   註解　輔助的 (形容詞)

1612. The report changed the **aspect** (view, appearance) of the situation.

   註解　外觀 (名詞)

1613. The birds **gorged** (ate a great deal greedily) on the cherries.

   註解　貪吃 (動詞)

1614. A **deceptive** (misleading) smile hid the man's anger.

   註解　虛僞的 (形容詞)

1615. The new student has only a **rudimentary** (beginning, of an early stage) knowledge of chemistry.

   註解　初步的 (形容詞)

1616. The examination tested the **sensory** (relating to the senses) reactions of the patient.

   註解　感覺上的 (形容詞)

1617. During the summer the noise of the **cicadas** (locusts) seems to make us aware of the heat.

   註解　蟬 (名詞)

1618. An **acute** (keen, sharp) sense of smell warned the woman of the fire.

   註解　刺鼻的 (形容詞)

1619. In a few words the speaker sketched **vignettes** (pictures) of the Mexican villages he had visited.

   註解　小插圖 (名詞)

1620. Each **facet** (plane surface) of the diamond reflected light.

   註解　刻面 (名詞)

1621. The virus was so small as to be even **microscopically** (with a microscope) invisible.

   註解　顯微鏡地 (副詞)

1622. To the child a trip to the circus was a **titillating** (pleasurably exciting) experience.

    註解   刺激的 (形容詞)

1623. One hates to **contemplate** (think seriously about) the horrors of atomic warfare.

    註解   沉思 (不定詞)

1624. That the detectives had not **fathomed** (understood, penetrated) the mystery angered the police captain.

    註解   徹底明白 (動詞，完成式)

1625. At the picnic ants swarmed over everything **edible** (eatable).

    註解   可吃的 (形容詞)

1626. The explorer told **incredible** (unbelievable) tales of his adventures.

    註解   難相信的 (形容詞)

1627. In spite of **ingenious** (clever) excuses the boy had to write the report.

    註解   精巧的 (形容詞)

1628. A **composite** (made up of different parts) picture often distorts the truth.

    註解   湊成的 (形容詞)

1629. The weight lifter performed **prodigies** (extraordinary deeds, marvels) of strength.

    註解   驚人之事 (名詞)

1630. The **tympanic** (part of the ear) membrane is part of one of the sense organs.

    註解   中耳的 (形容詞)

1631. Her father gave her **lavish** (extravagant) gifts on every holiday.

    註解   耗費的 (形容詞)

1632. I could not remember one answer; my mind had become a **vacuum** (space entirely empty of all matter).

    註解   眞空 (名詞)

1633. Most animals make **adaptations** (changes) to new situations.

    註解   適應 (名詞)

1634. Race car designers should be experts in the field **dynamics** (field of mechanics dealing with motion of bodies).

    註解   動力學 (名詞)

1635. Across the toe of the shoe was a row of **perforations** (small holes).
　　　 註解　小洞 (名詞)

1636. **Migratory** (moving from one place to another) workers usually have undesirable living conditions.
　　　 註解　流動的 (形容詞)

1637. One could almost look through the **fragile** (delicate, easily broken) china cup.
　　　 註解　易碎的 (形容詞)

1638. The intense heat caused a **buckling** (crumpling up, bending) of the steel plates in the boiler.
　　　 註解　膨脹 (動名詞)

1639. The **tubular** (like a tube) legs of the chair were made of steel.
　　　 註解　管狀的 (形容詞)

1640. Because of the work of **entomologists** (those who study insect life) many plant pests have been controlled.
　　　 註解　昆蟲學家 (名詞)

1641. Far out on the lake the sailors saw the **beacon** (guiding signal).
　　　 註解　燈塔，信號 (名詞)

1642. The lawyers and the jury rose **simultaneously** (at the same time) when the judge entered the room.
　　　 註解　同時地 (副詞)

1643. As children, we liked to play in the **cupola** (small dome on roof) on Grandmother's house.
　　　 註解　閣樓 (名詞)

1644. The light cast **grotesque** (unnatural, appearing, queer) shadows on the wall.
　　　 註解　古怪的 (形容詞)

1645. The **passive** (lacking will to act) attitude of the boy toward his school work irritated his ambitious parents.
　　　 註解　消極的 (形容詞)

1646. The **harried** (exhausted, tormented by tasks) mother no sooner quieted one twin than the other began to cry.
　　　 註解　苦惱的 (形容詞)

1647. Bits of **flotsam** (drifting persons or things) led the rescue party to the ship.

　　註解　漂浮之人或物 (名詞)

1648. The crowd **taunted** (made sarcastic remarks to) the star player who struck out.

　　註解　痛罵 (動詞)

1649. Before the bombing, the town was **evacuated** (emptied).

　　註解　清空 (動詞，被動式)

1650. After the explosion objects went **hurtling** (rushing) through the air in all directions.

　　註解　碰撞 (動名詞)

1651. The fighter exhibited **prodigious** (great in size or quantity) strength.

　　註解　驚人的，巨大的 (形容詞)

1652. The work of a poet is **comparable** (similar) in many ways to the work of an artist.

　　註解　可相比的 (形容詞)

1653. The correspondent hastily **dispatched** (sent) news of the victory to his paper.

　　註解　發送 (動詞)

1654. The hearse stopped briefly at the **crematorium** (place where corpses are reduced to ashes).

　　註解　火葬場 (名詞，同 crematory)

1655. **Prodigal** (Extravagant) sums were spent on the dance decorations.

　　註解　奢侈的 (形容詞)

1656. All the boats on the **lagoon** (shallow lake) eagerly waited for the start of the race.

　　註解　小湖 (名詞，同 lagune)

1657. The losing team **despondently** (in low spirits) filed off the field.

　　註解　沮喪地 (副詞)

1658. **Comparative** (some degree of) quiet reigned after the confusion of the pep meeting.

　　註解　比較的 (形容詞)

1659. The **debauched** (wicked, immoral) court of the king caused the people to revolt.

　　　| 註解 |　荒淫的 (形容詞)

1660. From the **vantage** (position giving superiority) of the broadcasting booth we could see the game clearly.

　　　| 註解 |　優越之位置 (名詞)

1661. The **staccato** (with sharp, disconnected sounds) barking of a dog awakened us.

　　　| 註解 |　斷音的 (形容詞)

1662. Peeping through the trees, the children saw **lurid** (horrible, ghostly) figures dancing around the fire.

　　　| 註解 |　恐怖的 (形容詞)

1663. The blazing apartment house became a(n) **inferno** (scene resembling hell).

　　　| 註解 |　地獄 (名詞)

1664. Because we had no **kindling** (easily lighted material), we had difficulty starting the fire.

　　　| 註解 |　易燃物 (動名詞)

1665. The riders **cantered** (galloped easily) through the park enjoying the beautiful gardens.

　　　| 註解 |　慢跑 (動詞)

1666. The **cayuse** (Indian pony) was found wandering down the canyon.

　　　| 註解 |　小野馬 (名詞)

1667. Although rather large, the **roan** (horse) was the first pet the boy ever owned.

　　　| 註解 |　雜色馬 (名詞)

1668. The vice-president was an **eminent** (distinguished) man.

　　　| 註解 |　聞名的 (形容詞)

1669. The **cavalry** (mounted soldiers) was some distance away.

　　　| 註解 |　騎兵 (名詞)

1670. The villains' **exploits** (daring deeds) were widely known.

　　　| 註解 |　功績 (名詞)

1671. His **Spartan** (simple and severe) life was amazing.

　　　| 註解 |　斯巴達式的，剛勇的 (形容詞)

1672. The **paradox** (situation full of contradictions) was very thought-provoking.

   註解　相互矛盾的話 (名詞)

1673. The admiral steered an **eccentric** (odd) course.

   註解　古怪的 (形容詞)

1674. The situation was **horrendous** (frightful).

   註解　恐怖的 (形容詞)

1675. The **secession** (act of withdrawing from) was an orderly affair.

   註解　退出(名詞)

1676. He was a **pathetic** (pitiful) figure.

   註解　悲慘的 (形容詞)

1677. It appeared to be a **fledgling** (young and inexperienced).

   註解　年輕無經驗的 (名詞)

1678. Her **tactical** (cleverness about military planning) knowledge surprised everyone.

   註解　戰術的 (形容詞)

1679. The man's **peer** (equal) had vanished.

   註解　同輩 (名詞)

1680. He spoke in a **brash** (reckless) manner.

   註解　粗魯的 (形容詞)

1681. The coyote was quite **aggressive** (bold).

   註解　侵略性的 (形容詞)

1682. These are people of my **generation** (of the same period of time).

   註解　同世代的人 (名詞)

1683. The orator **waxed** (became forceful in speaking) eloquent at the end.

   註解　增大 (動詞)

1684. The team was highly **touted** (praised).

   註解　稱讚的 (形容詞)

1685. The **phenomenon** (something extraordinary) has caused much comment.

   註解　現象 (名詞)

1686. The trouble was **reminiscent** (recalling the past) of an earlier time.

   註解　回憶的 (形容詞)

1687. The trial was a fine **endeavor** (effort).

   註解　努力 (名詞)

1688. His **lethargy** (inactivity) was apparent.

　　　註解　昏睡 (名詞)

1689. He is a **virile** (vigorous) person.

　　　註解　剛健的 (形容詞)

1690. It was a feat of **derring-do** (daring deeds).

　　　註解　大膽行為 (名詞)

1691. The **strategy** (planning) was carefully timed.

　　　註解　策略 (名詞)

1692. Next came a(n) **indictment** (charging with doing wrong) of athletics.

　　　註解　控告 (名詞)

1693. He did not have enough **stamina** (endurance).

　　　註解　精力 (名詞)

1694. This activity is only **intramural** (within a school).

　　　註解　校內的 (形容詞)

1695. The new building has better **facilities** (conveniences).

　　　註解　設備 (名詞)

1696. He regards school clubs as **adjuncts** (helpful but not necessary).

　　　註解　附屬的 (名詞)

1697. Another speaker reported on **secondary schools** (high schools)

　　　註解　中學 (名詞)

1698. They prefer someone with an **agile** (lively and quick) mind.

　　　註解　活潑的 (形容詞)

1699. We were impressed by the **coordination** (working together of parts).

　　　註解　調和 (名詞)

1700. The child's **physique** (body development) was good.

　　　註解　體格 (名詞)

1701. 1701.The **deterioration** (becoming worse) was saddening.

　　　註解　變壞 (名詞)

1702. The younger men tend to be **effete** (sarcastic).

　　　註解　疲憊的，諷刺的 (形容詞)

1703. Here is a **specimen** (example) of the material.

　　　註解　樣品 (名詞)

1704. He was **intrigued** (interested) to learn of it.

　　　註解　感興趣 (動詞，被動式)

1705. The reporter gave an **unbiased** (fair account) version.

　　註解　公平的 (形容詞)

1706. The **spectator** (one who observes) cheered the player.

　　註解　觀眾 (名詞)

1707. In the spring we wanted to **return** (go back) to the mountains.

　　註解　返回 (不定詞)

1708. Keeping house is **new** (unfamiliar) to her.

　　註解　不熟悉的 (形容詞)

1709. The **eye** (hole) of the needles is too small.

　　註解　孔，洞 (名詞)

1710. Almost everyone **appreciated** (was grateful for) the play.

　　註解　欣賞 (動詞)

1711. After the flood the river will **fall** (descend) six feet.

　　註解　降下 (動詞)

1712. When she fell she got a **run** (ravel) in her stocking.

　　註解　脫線 (名詞)

1713. The captain is **fretful** (fearful) because his compass is broken.

　　註解　焦急的 (形容詞)

1714. It took a **game** (plucky) boy to ride that horse.

　　註解　有膽量的 (形容詞)

1715. He was in **command** (mandate) of the ship.

　　註解　操控 (名詞)

1716. He is not ready to **command** (control) a large salary.

　　註解　控制 (不定詞)

1717. The farmer will **bed down** (provide with a bed to) his animals.

　　註解　鋪床 (動詞片語)

1718. She could do many tricks on the **bar** (rod).

　　註解　桿子 (名詞)

1719. They had to hunt **games** (animals) for their food.

　　註解　獵物 (名詞)

1720. Play the last **bar** (measure) of music again.

　　註解　韻律，音樂一小節 (名詞)

1721. That family has a large **circle** (coterie) of friends.

　　註解　團體 (名詞)

1722. I will have to **draw** (take) some money from the bank.

   註解　提取 (不定詞)

1723. We heat houses by the **combustion** (flame) of coal.

   註解　燃燒 (名詞)

1724. **Gradually** (Slowly) he learned to read.

   註解　漸漸地 (副詞)

1725. The puppy ran **hither and thither** (here and there).

   註解　到處 (副詞片語)

1726. The children were **desperate** (grave)when the baby fell in the water.

   註解　危險的 (形容詞)

1727. The dog was **accustomed** (used) to just one meal a day.

   註解　習慣 (動詞，被動式)

1728. After the **completion** (fulfillment) of this job, what will you do?

   註解　完成 (名詞)

1729. The children were **extremely** (exceedingly) helpful on the day of the picnic.

   註解　非常地 (副詞)

1730. The scene exhibit made us **marvelous** (wonderful).

   註解　奇異的 (形容詞)

1731. The house **adjacent** (neighboring) to ours is painted red.

   註解　緊鄰的 (形容詞)

1732. The dog regarded the postman with **suspicion** (mistrust).

   註解　懷疑 (名詞)

1733. For me, it was a **tedious** (monotonous) task.

   註解　乏味的，單調的 (形容詞)

1734. The noise of the fireworks **enraged** (maddened) the dog.

   註解　激怒 (動詞)

1735. I do not like **violent** (furious) language.

   註解　激烈的 (形容詞)

1736. The **habitat** (quarter) of the fern is in the cool woods.

   註解　棲息地 (名詞)

1737. She thought a new dress was **indispensable** (requisite).

   註解　不可缺少的 (形容詞)

1738. I saw the movie twice because it **entranced** (enraptured) me.

　　註解　使高興 (動詞)

1739. The little boy had **hazel** (reddish-brown) eyes.

　　註解　淡褐色的 (形容詞)

1740. Because she saved the child, they called her a **heroine** (female hero).

　　註解　女英雄 (名詞)

1741. The boy found some **jaspers** (stoneware) on his vacation.

　　註解　次寶石 (名詞)

1742. The **impetus** (impulse) of the water washed the wall away.

　　註解　衝力 (名詞)

1743. The child loved her **kaleidoscope** (optical instrument).

　　註解　萬花筒，視力工具 (名詞)

1744. Can they **justify** (vindicate) spending so much money?

　　註解　辯解 (動詞)

1745. Will you **accompany** (attend) me on the trip?

　　註解　參加 (動詞)

1746. **Apparently** (Conspicuously) the children are having fun.

　　註解　顯然地 (副詞)

1747. The boys **beheld** (discerned) the circus posters with glee.

　　註解　注視 (動詞)

1748. **Frequently** (Often) they went swimming in the pool.

　　註解　經常地 (副詞)

1749. He had a(n) **opportunity** (chance) to go to the circus.

　　註解　機會 (名詞)

1750. Her **portrait** (picture) was hanging in the hall.

　　註解　肖像 (名詞)

1751. We were all **bewitched** (enchanted) by the television show.

　　註解　陶醉 (動詞，被動式)

1752. He was **bewailing** (bemoaning) his failure in the examination.

　　註解　嘆息的 (形容詞)

1753. I would not care to be called **indolent** (slothful) because I would be lazy.

　　註解　懶惰的 (形容詞)

1754. I would like to be called **loyal** because I would be (faithful).

　　註解　忠誠的 (形容詞)

1755. I would like to be called jocund because I would be (gay).

   註解　高興的 (形容詞)

1756. I would not care to be called **languid** because I would be (slack).

   註解　不活潑的 (形容詞)

1757. I would like to be called **judicious** because I would be (rational).

   註解　明智的 (形容詞)

1758. I would not care to be called **truant** because I would be (idle).

   註解　遊蕩的 (形容詞)

1759. I would not care to be called **lawless** because I would be (unruly).

   註解　不守法的 (形容詞)

1760. I would not care to be called **impertinent** because I would be (impudent).

   註解　粗暴的 (形容詞)

1761. I would like to be called **diligent** because I would be (sedulous).

   註解　勤勉的 (形容詞)

1762. I would not care to be called **loutish** because I would be (boorish).

   註解　粗野的 (形容詞)

1763. I would like to be called **knightly** because I would be (brave).

   註解　勇敢的 (形容詞)

1764. I would like to be called **liberal** because I would be (charitable).

   註解　大方的 (形容詞)

1765. I would not care to be called **insolent** because I would be (brazen-faced).

   註解　粗野的 (形容詞)

1766. I would not care to be called **belligerent** because I would be (bellicose).

   註解　好戰的 (形容詞)

1767. I would like to be called **generous** because I would be (unstinting).

   註解　慷慨的 (形容詞)

1768. I would not care to be called **ludicrous** because I would be (farcical).

   註解　可笑的 (形容詞)

1769. I would like to be called a **benefactor** because I would be a (kindly helper).

   註解　施主 (名詞)

1770. I would like to be called **bountiful** because I would be (munificent).

   註解　大方的 (形容詞)

1771. The woman **yelled** (said) at us.

   註解　呼喊 (動詞)

1772. Jim is an (a) **smart** (intelligent) boy.

   註解　聰明的 (形容詞)

1773. Your dad was **unpleasant** (angry).

   註解　生氣的 (形容詞)

1774. He **protected** (maintained) his rights.

   註解　維護 (動詞)

1775. The ghost has **disappeared** (vanished).

   註解　消失的 (形容詞)

1776. Nursing is a good **career** (job).

   註解　工作 (名詞)

1777. 1777.The **breeze** (wind) feels cool.

   註解　風吹 (名詞)

1778. Everyone remained **silent** (quiet).

   註解　安靜的 (形容詞)

1779. Sally **wept** (cried).

   註解　哭泣 (動詞)

1780. The problem was **easy** (simple).

   註解　簡單的 (形容詞)

1781. It's **cool** (chilly) in here.

   註解　有點冷的 (形容詞)

1782. Do you have any **hints** (ideas)?

   註解　提示 (名詞)

1783. The new girl is **timid** (shy).

   註解　害羞的 (形容詞)

1784. We need to buy a **present** (gift).

   註解　禮物 (名詞)

1785. The class is going on a **hike** (walk).

   註解　遠足 (名詞)

1786. The **nightmare** (dream) was terrible.

   註解　惡夢 (名詞)

1787. The **gem** (jewel) sparkled.

   註解　寶石 (名詞)

1788. The paint was **smudged** (spotted).

   註解　污點的 (形容詞)

1789. He **patted** (touched) the dog on the head.

   註解　輕拍 (動詞)

1790. You should find this task very **manageable** (controllable).

   註解　可處理的 (形容詞)

1791. A burning arrow was **shot** (sent) with speed onto the roof of the log house inthe clearing.

   註解　射出 (動詞，被動式)

1792. The mountain climbers crawled inch by inch toward toe ice-capped **tip** (peak) high above them.

   註解　頂點 (名詞)

1793. When the soldier **inquired** (asked), the captain explained why he would never order his men to fire on that village.

   註解　要求 (動詞)

1794. Not one of the campers thought it was too trouble be travel fifty miles just to see a **lot** (herd) of buffaloes.

   註解　群 (名詞)

1795. The whole family thought that Father was clever to be able to make a strawberry shortcake that was so **delicious** (good).

   註解　美味的 (形容詞)

1796. Would you give our thanks to the brave boy who stayed with our son until he could **get loose** (escape) from the fierce net of seaweed?

   註解　逃脫 (動詞片語)

1797. When the signal tower on the beach fell, the cottages nearly began to shake and the people began to **cry out** (squeal) in fright.

   註解　尖叫 (不定詞片語)

1798. Skip was happy when he could **float** (drift) about in his old rowboat and fancy himself as someday being head of a big ocean liner.

   註解　漂浮 (動詞)

1799. Ruth kept looking at the **bundle** (pack) of money she had discovered when she had put her hand into the hollow tree trunk.

   註解　束，包 (名詞)

1800. The telephone is a useful **invention** (devising).

   > 註解　發明(名詞)

1801. The dentist pulled my tooth, and to my surprise it was **painless** (tormentingless).

   > 註解　不痛的 (形容詞)

1802. The boys had a valuable coin **collection** (aggregation).

   > 註解　收集 (名詞)

1803. Tim's only **objection** (opposition) was that the sweater cost too much.

   > 註解　反對 (名詞)

1804. I saw my **reflection** (reflexion) in the water.

   > 註解　倒影 (名詞)

1805. The **adoption** (taking as one's own child) agency found parents for the homeless child.

   > 註解　收養 (名詞)

1806. The **squabble** (spat) did not last long.

   > 註解　小爭吵 (名詞)

1807. We expect a very large **multitude** (horde)

   > 註解　群眾 (名詞)

1808. The **greenhorn** (apprentice) was rather clumsy.

   > 註解　無經驗的人 (名詞)

1809. Medicines helped to ease the **distress** (misery).

   > 註解　痛苦 (名詞)

1810. We are ready to begin the **excursion** (expedition).

   > 註解　旅行 (名詞)

1811. He receives his **remuneration** (earnings).

   > 註解　報酬 (名詞)

1812. The **hubbub** (tumult) gave me a headache.

   > 註解　喧嘩 (名詞)

1813. Their **genius** (knack) for cooking is amazing.

   > 註解　天才，技巧 (名詞)

1814. There is too much **animosity** (rancor) between us.

   > 註解　仇恨 (名詞)

1815. Nobody wanted the **surplus** (leftovers).

   > 註解　剩飯，剩菜

1816. Was anyone hurt in the **melee** (scuffle)?

    > 註解　亂打，混戰 (名詞)

1817. A new **abode** (mansion) is being built here.

    > 註解　住處，大廈 (名詞)

1818. It is a **facsimile** (replica) of an antique car.

    > 註解　複製品 (名詞)

1819. The **pact** (covenant) we made is fair.

    > 註解　協定 (名詞)

1820. I admire my **adversary's** (rival's) courage.

    > 註解　仇敵，對手 (名詞)

1821. It's our duty to obey the **edict** (decree).

    > 註解　佈告 (名詞)

1822. We escaped during the **bedlam** (pandemonium).

    > 註解　騷亂 (名詞)

1823. "A penny saved is a penny earned" is a famous **maxim** (adage).

    > 註解　格言 (名詞)

1824. They had a great **hankering** (yearning) to go home.

    > 註解　渴望 (名詞)

1825. I am a **partisan** (disciple) of Senator Jones.

    > 註解　同黨，信徒 (名詞)

1826. I think he is a big **faker** (mountebank).

    > 註解　騙子 (名詞)

1827. We prevented a serious **mishap** (catastrophe).

    > 註解　災難 (名詞)

1828. The new **potentate** (monarch) was crowned today.

    > 註解　統治者 (名詞)

1829. We found **sanctuary** (haven) in a small cave.

    > 註解　聖堂，避難所 (名詞)

1830. We had a very interesting **parley** (discourse)

    > 註解　商議 (名詞)

1831. My **overseer** (supervision) is a very pleasant person.

    > 註解　監督者 (名詞)

1832. We have finally reached the **pinnacle** (apex).

    > 註解　苦惱 (動詞)

1833. Their loud talking **vexed** (irked) everyone.
> 註解　苦惱 (動詞)

1834. The new radio codes **perplexed** (muddled) the pilot.
> 註解　迷惑 (動詞)

1835. They were **eulogized** (acclaimed) for their deeds.
> 註解　讚揚 (動詞，被動式)

1836. The sly quarterback **duped** (deluded) our team.
> 註解　欺騙 (動詞)

1837. After two hours, the storm **lessened** (ebbed).
> 註解　變小 (動詞)

1838. I was **flabbergasted** (dumfounded) by your masks.
> 註解　驚呆 (動詞，被動式)

1839. The careless guard was **reviled** (chastised).
> 註解　辱罵 (動詞，被動式)

1840. We were **ashamed** (humiliated) when we dropped it.
> 註解　慚愧的 (形容詞)

1841. "Save us!" **supplicated** (implored) the sinking men.
> 註解　懇求 (動詞)

1842. Then I heard someone **snicker** (chortle).
> 註解　暗笑 (名詞)

1843. They tried to **plunder** (purloin) her jewels.
> 註解　搶奪 (不定詞)

1844. This will **thwart** (impede) bike riding here.
> 註解　妨礙 (動詞)

1845. Contemplate (Meditate) for a while before you decide.
> 註解　考慮 (動詞)

1846. We will **obliterate** (demolish) the enemy fort.
> 註解　消滅 (動詞)

1847. We'll **ostracize** (eject) them from our club.
> 註解　逐出 (動詞)

1848. The young people **idolize** (adore) them.
> 註解　崇拜 (動詞)

1849. Members voted to **revoke** (nullify) the rule.
> 註解　廢棄 (不定詞)

1850. Can you **accumulate** (assemble) a stack of acorns?

註解　堆積 (動詞)

1851. We **veto** (forbid) chewing gum in school.

註解　禁止 (動詞)

1852. Then the bridge began to **quake** (quiver).

註解　搖動 (不定詞)

1853. We saw him **saunter** (amble) down the street.

註解　閒逛 (名詞)

1854. How did you **kindle** (singe) the towel?

註解　引起燃燒 (動詞)

1855. They soon might **defeat** (quell) cancer.

註解　擊敗 (動詞)

1856. Finally, they had to **capitulate** (submit).

註解　投降 (不定詞)

1857. You shouldn't **mock** (ridicule) the deaf girl.

註解　嘲弄 (動詞)

1858. Actors must **scrutinize** (scan) their lines daily.

註解　細查 (動詞)

1859. They said she is an **exquisite** (gorgeous) girl.

註解　華麗的 (形容詞)

1860. Bob's father is an **adroit** (deft) juggler.

註解　機巧的 (形容詞)

1861. The lights on the tree are **scintillating** (dazzling).

註解　閃耀的 (形容詞)

1862. It is very **tranquil** (serene) in the mountains.

註解　平靜的 (形容詞)

1863. Their shortstop is very **scrawny** (rangy).

註解　細長的 (形容詞)

1864. We protested the **barbaric** (brutal) punishment.

註解　野蠻的 (形容詞)

1865. Then we found a **veiled** (cryptic) trail.

註解　隱蔽的 (形容詞)

1866. I think she is too **pompous** (conceited).

註解　誇大的 (形容詞)

1867. That is a very **affable** (genial) family.

> 註解 　和藹的 (形容詞)

1868. He told us the water is **contaminated** (adulterated).

> 註解 　污染的 (形容詞)

1869. Who made that **ludicrous** (nonsensical) remark.

> 註解 　荒謬的 (形容詞)

1870. The **constant** (incessant) noise made my head ache.

> 註解 　不斷的 (形容詞)

1871. A **loathsome** (repulsive) creature frightened us.

> 註解 　討厭的 (形容詞)

1872. The driver of the car is **infuriated** (furious).

> 註解 　狂怒的 (形容詞)

1873. Poor losers say umpires are **prejudiced** (unjust).

> 註解 　偏見的 (形容詞)

1874. The chef prepared a **toothsome** (luscious) meal.

> 註解 　明智的 (形容詞)

1875. Your decision is very **sage** (prudent) one.

> 註解 　味美的 (形容詞)

1876. The students are very **jittery** (jumpy).

> 註解 　神經質的 (形容詞)

1877. We rowed through a **dreary** (dismal) swamp.

> 註解 　淒涼的 (形容詞)

1878. Susan is such a **dynamic** (energetic) girl.

> 註解 　精力充沛的 (形容詞)

1879. The **plump** (obese) man was ordered to diet.

> 註解 　圓胖的 (形容詞)

1880. The old bridge is **perilous** (hazardous).

> 註解 　危險的 (形容詞)

1881. These problems are **trifling** (trivial).

> 註解 　不重要的 (形容詞)

1882. I escaped from a **stinking** (malodorous) dungeon.

> 註解 　臭味的 (形容詞)

1883. She often gives **peculiar** (eccentric) answers.

> 註解 　奇異的 (形容詞)

1884. We welcomed the **renowned** (celebrated) scientist.

> 註解　著名的 (形容詞)

1885. He was fired for being **slipshod** (lax).

> 註解　懶散的 (形容詞)

1886. Everyone is very **grouchy** (cross) today.

> 註解　不悅的 (形容詞)

1887. The **spunky** (dauntless) youth was honored.

> 註解　勇敢的 (形容詞)

1888. Carry the **frail** (puny), old soldier inside.

> 註解　衰弱的 (形容詞)

1889. Trudy dislikes her **monotonous** (humdrum) job.

> 註解　單調的 (形容詞)

1890. His clothes are torn and **filthy** (sordid).

> 註解　不乾淨的 (形容詞)

1891. We destroyed the **venomous** (noxious) liquid.

> 註解　有毒的 (形容詞)

1892. The team is **jubilant** (blissful) because they won.

> 註解　歡欣的 (形容詞)

1893. Police captured the **maniacal** (deranged) killer.

> 註解　瘋狂的 (形容詞)

1894. Our food supply is **lavish** (copious).

> 註解　豐富的 (形容詞)

1895. The **cantankerous** (stubborn) boy will not help us.

> 註解　懷脾氣的 (形容詞)

1896. Two **potent** (burl) men carried the dog.

> 註解　有力的 (形容詞)

1897. The **tense** (anxious) coach sat on the bench.

> 註解　緊張的 (形容詞)

1898. The dinner was **superb** (splendid).

> 註解　豐盛的 (形容詞)

1899. **Avid** (Zealous) supporters cheered the team.

> 註解　熱誠的 (形容詞)

1900. Your friend is very **gracious** (courteous).

> 註解　親切的 (形容詞)

1901. Their feats are truly **miraculous** (fabulous).

> 註解　神奇的 (形容詞)

1902. We ignored the **insolent** (impudent) guests.

> 註解　粗魯的 (形容詞)

1903. He is wearing a **vermilion** (crimson) jacket.

> 註解　朱紅色的 (形容詞)

1904. After the flood, we were **indigent** (impoverished).

> 註解　貧乏的 (形容詞)

1905. The smoke makes objects **obscure** (indistinct).

> 註解　模糊的 (形容詞)

1906. Many of the **dehydrated** (arid) plants are dead.

> 註解　枯乾的 (形容詞)

1907. They were caught by a **nefarious** (sinful) witch.

> 註解　邪惡的 (形容詞)

1908. I'm **weary** (fatigued) after that long hike.

> 註解　疲勞的 (形容詞)

1909. We were **doleful** (glum) when our friend left.

> 註解　憂愁的 (形容詞)

1910. The **merciful** (compassionate) judge pardoned them.

> 註解　仁慈的 (形容詞)

1911. He is **parsimonious** (selfish) with his money.

> 註解　吝嗇的 (形容詞)

1912. The boys think she is **winsome** (alluring).

> 註解　迷人的 (形容詞)

1913. The **gigantic** (mammoth) building blocked the wind.

> 註解　巨大的 (形容詞)

1914. All of us are very **repentant** (remorseful).

> 註解　悔恨的 (形容詞)

1915. The **sly** (cunning) thief was captured.

> 註解　狡猾的 (形容詞)

1916. His remarks are often **witty** (comical).

> 註解　詼諧的 (形容詞)

1917. **Sluggish** (Indolent) boys slept under the tree.

> 註解　懶惰的 (形容詞)

1918. This foul shot is **momentous** (vital).

> 註解 極重要的，致命的 (形容詞)

1919. We spent a(n) **amiable** (friendly) afternoon playing games.

> 註解 悅人的 (形容詞)

1920. A group of **brawny** (muscular) boys helped carry the boxes.

> 註解 強壯的 (形容詞)

1921. That slender lad is a very **canny** (prudent) pitcher.

> 註解 謹慎的 (形容詞)

1922. Every child in that family is **chivalrous** (valiant).

> 註解 俠義的 (形容詞)

1923. The scarf you knitted for father is **comely** (good-looking).

> 註解 漂亮的 (形容詞)

1924. I was **crestfallen** (dejected) when I saw my test score.

> 註解 氣餒的 (形容詞)

1925. We put a box of **desicated** (dehydrated) fruit in our boat.

> 註解 乾乾的 (形容詞)

1926. The **despondent** (disheartened) children watched it rained.

> 註解 消沉的 (形容詞)

1927. The **emaciated** (lean) man was wandering in the desert.

> 註解 瘦弱的 (形容詞)

1928. They are **exultant** (jubilant) because school is over.

> 註解 狂歡的 (形容詞)

1929. The **fagged** (exhausted) players trudged off the field.

> 註解 疲勞的 (形容詞)

1930. I laughed when the **haughty** (snobbish) boy fell in the mud.

> 註解 驕傲的 (形容詞)

1931. She has no friends because she is so **headstrong** (willful).

> 註解 任性的 (形容詞)

1932. The **heedless** (unmindful) boy crashed his bike into a pole.

> 註解 不注意的 (形容詞)

1933. She is **indignant** (wrathful) because I broke her pencil.

> 註解 憤慨的 (形容詞)

1934. My friend gave me some **sagacious** (enlightened) advice.

> 註解 開明的 (形容詞)

1935. We silently searched the **murky** (dim) cave.

註解　漆黑的 (形容詞)

1936. She said she had a **pacific** (gentle) ride on the plane.

註解　平穩的 (形容詞)

1937. The **perpetual** (everlasting) rains ruined our vacation.

註解　沒有間斷的 (形容詞)

1938. We tried to cheer up our **peevish** (petulant) classmate.

註解　暴躁的 (形容詞)

1939. Their players are huge, but ours are **plucky** (spunky).

註解　有膽量的 (形容詞)

1940. I've never seen such **radiant** (refulgent) teeth as she has.

註解　閃亮的 (形容詞)

1941. The **rotund** (plump) boy can hit, but he's a slow runner.

註解　圓胖的 (形容詞)

1942. The footprints were **shrouded** (screened) by the bushes.

註解　覆蓋 (動詞，被動式)

1943. Their **sinister** (wicked) plan was unsuccessful.

註解　邪惡的 (形容詞)

1944. The pact we made today should end the **controversy** (dispute).

註解　爭論 (名詞)

1945. "Ignorance of the law," is an old **platitude** (epigram).

註解　警語 (名詞)

1946. The scientist and his **advocate** (adherent) receives no salary.

註解　擁護者 (名詞)

1947. The clamor from the **skirmish** (combat) awoke the prince.

註解　小爭論 (名詞)

1948. Our greatest **hunger** (yen) is to have an abode of our own.

註解　願望 (名詞)

1949. A passenger in the train accident is in great **torment** (anguish).

註解　痛苦 (名詞)

1950. The **novice** (rookie) started his long climb to the peak.

註解　新手 (名詞)

1951. He has a talent for making things out of the **remnants** (residues).

註解　殘餘物 (名詞)

1952. This is a **duplicate** (imitation) of our enemy's uniform.
　　　註解　複製品 (名詞)

1953. The mob chased the **phony** (quack) out of the village.
　　　註解　冒充者 (名詞)

1954. We found **refuge** (shelter) in a barn during our journey.
　　　註解　避難所 (名詞)

1955. The slaves were filled with **malice** (hostility) toward the king.
　　　註解　惡意 (名詞)

1956. The boss managed to halt the **uproar** (chaos) in the mill.
　　　註解　騷動 (名詞)

1957. You are trying to **swindle** (gyp) me.
　　　註解　欺騙 (不定詞)

1958. An **ordinance** (A statue) forbids dumping the residue into the lake.
　　　註解　法令 (名詞)

1959. The neophyte receives less **stipend** (wages) than we do.
　　　註解　薪水 (名詞)

1960. Supporters of the team planned a **jaunt** (trek) to the game.
　　　註解　旅行 (名詞)

1961. The artist's a fraud and his painting is a replica (facsimile).
　　　註解　摹實品 (名詞)

1962. It began as a mild **argument** (quarrel) but turned into a fight.
　　　註解　爭吵 (名詞)

1963. The **sovereign** (emperor) was fond of quoting old proverb.
　　　註解　君主 (名詞)

1964. Our **employer** (foreman) has a craving for jelly doughnuts.
　　　註解　工頭 (名詞)

1965. What caused the confusion among the **aggregation** (throng)?
　　　註解　群眾 (名詞)

1966. What discourse was interrupted by the **din** (clamor).
　　　註解　喧嘩 (名詞)

1967. I will use my **aptitude** (flair) to fight distress and malice.
　　　註解　才能 (名詞)

1968. The **neophyte** (amateur) was told to study the rule.
　　　註解　生手 (名詞)

1969. If there is no **calamity** (disaster), we will so be at the apex.
    註解　災難 (名詞)

1970. The knight's fleeing **antagonist** (foe) sought sanctuary here.
    註解　敵手 (名詞)

1971. We must **venerate** (bar) their plan to wreck the palace.
    註解　阻止 (動詞)

1972. The boy was scolded because he had **irritated** (disturbed) the guests.
    註解　妨害 (動詞，完成式)

1973. The natives gather here to **glorify** (worship) their gods.
    註解　崇拜 (不定詞)

1974. They **misled** (fooled) us and then they embarrassed us.
    註解　誤導 (動詞)

1975. The audience began to **titter** (giggle) and to mock the juggler.
    註解　竊笑 (不定詞)

1976. They should **repeal** (abolish) the rule that forbids dancing.
    註解　廢止 (動詞)

1977. His decision to surrender **astounded** (startled) his opponent.
    註解　吃驚 (動詞)

1978. After you examine the secret maps, you must **scorch** (sear) them.
    註解　大罵 (動詞)

1979. We will **banish** (exclude) any member who tries to cheat anyone.
    註解　驅逐 (動詞)

1980. After the applause dwindled, she was **lauded** (complimented) even more.
    註解　讚美 (動詞，被動式)

1981. When the walls began to shake, we were **bewildered** (baffled).
    註解　昏亂的 (形容詞)

1982. If your defeat me, I will **plod** (stride) through that snowdrift.
    註解　行走 (動詞)

1983. "Don't incinerate our ship!" **entreated** (pleaded) the sailors.
    註解　乞求 (動詞)

1984. Our hopes had **diminished** (dwindled), so we had to capitulate.
    註解　縮減 (動詞，完成式)

1985. My lawyer will impede them if they try to **fleece** (rook) us.
    註解　詐取 (不定詞)

1986. Scrutinize this carefully and then **ravage** (exterminate) it.
　　註解　破壞 (動詞)

1987. If we **ponder** (reflect), perhaps we can quell the mosquitoes.
　　註解　想一想 (動詞)

1988. You will be **reprimanded** (chided) if you ridicule the new pupil.
　　註解　懲處 (動詞，被動式)

1989. If we **outlaw** (ban) parking here, drivers will be bewildered.
　　註解　禁止 (動詞)

1990. A fence will hinder any attempt to **filch** (pilfer) our flowers.
　　註解　偷竊 (不定詞)

1991. I'm going to **compile** (gather) my baseball cards and peruse them.
　　註解　收集 (不定詞)

1992. The tired explorers made a **fantastic** (remarkable) discovery.
　　註解　奇異的 (形容詞)

1993. You were **sensible** (intelligent) not to argue with the stubborn clerk.
　　註解　聰明的 (形容詞)

1994. The evil knight fled into the **gloomy** (bleak) forest.
　　註解　幽暗的 (形容詞)

1995. Those **brilliant** (glittering) lights creates a constant glare.
　　註解　光輝的 (形容詞)

1996. Eager workers began cleaning the **tainted** (impure) creek.
　　註解　污點的 (形容詞)

1997. It is very important that we don't become **reckless** (neglectful).
　　註解　不留心的 (形容詞)

1998. The **noted** (distinguished) author's speech was excellent.
　　註解　著名的 (形容詞)

1999. Two strong umpires separated the **enraged** (irate) players.
　　註解　激怒的 (形容詞)

2000. The food at the party was plentiful and **delectable** (tasty).
　　註解　味美的 (形容詞)

2001. We were happy when the **valiant** (courageous) pilot was saved.
　　註解　勇敢的 (形容詞)

2002. The meaning of this **odd** (abnormal) message is unclear.
　　註解　奇怪的 (形容詞)

2003. I agree that he is amusing, but he is also **arrogant** (vain).
   註解　自大的 (形容詞)

2004. An eager collector found a **first-rate** (extraordinary) seashell.
   註解　特別的 (形容詞)

2005. A **sociable** (engaging) zookeeper greeted the lively children.
   註解　友善的 (形容詞)

2006. The kind girl cared for the **gaunt** (slender), weak chick.
   註解　細瘦的 (形容詞)

2007. A grouchy lady said the paintings were **gruesome** (unsightly).
   註解　可怕的 (形容詞)

2008. He stays **soothing** (peaceful) by ignoring unimportant complaints.
   註解　緩和的 (形容詞)

2009. The clever magician turns **putrid** (rancid) weeds into roses.
   註解　腐壞的 (形容詞)

2010. The big, snow-capped mountain is **attractive** (lovely).
   註解　吸引人的 (形容詞)

2011. The hot, **harsh** (savage) wind swept over the dry desert.
   註解　殘酷的 (形容詞)

2012. This is a **drab** (dull) book because the story is unclear.
   註解　單調的 (形容詞)

2013. We held a **covert** (concealed) meeting in a lonely, dreary cave.
   註解　暗地的 (形容詞)

2014. If you are smart, you won't try the **risky** (dangerous) leap.
   註解　危險的 (形容詞)

2015. They are strange because birds make them **fidgety** (impatient).
   註解　煩躁的 (形容詞)

2016. The well-known leader escaped from the **slovenly** (grimy) prison.
   註解　疏忽的 (形容詞)

2017. The courteous host gave us some hot, **sturdy** (mighty) coffee.
   註解　強烈的 (形容詞)

2018. I crept by the negligent guard into the **colossal** (enormous) castle.
   註解　巨大的 (形容詞)

2019. One **peppery** (spirited) child fell into the malodorous pond.
   註解　暴躁的 (形容詞)

2020. She is **captivating** (bewitching) and has a very engaging smile.

   註解　迷人的 (形容詞)

2021. Why are you so infuriated about a **petty** (minor) error?

   註解　細小的 (形容詞)

2022. The grass is **parched** (withered) and the river is contaminated.

   註解　枯萎的 (形容詞)

2023. The closefisted man wouldn't help the **melancholy** (needy) orphan.

   註解　悲哀的 (形容詞)

2024. Their arrogant leader lost the **crucial** (prodigious) election.

   註解　重要的 (形容詞)

2025. The repentant girl apologized for being **disrespectful** (rude).

   註解　無禮的 (形容詞)

2026. I think that garish **carmine** (scarlet) building is repulsive.

   註解　深紅色的 (形容詞)

2027. Those boys are never **cranky** (surly) or downhearted.

   註解　任性的 (形容詞)

2028. The cunning mice avoided the **lethal** (toxic) mousetrap.

   註解　有毒致命的 (形容詞)

2029. The **demented** (insane) witch pursued the fretful children.

   註解　瘋狂的 (形容詞)

2030. My **absurd** (ridiculous) remark made the exhausted king irate.

   註解　荒謬的 (形容詞)

2031. The **persistent** (uninterrupted) factory smoke makes our town grimy.

   註解　繼續不斷的 (形容詞)

2032. The **corrupt** (depraved) witch mixed a rancid, noxious potion.

   註解　敗壞的 (形容詞)

2033. After I made fun of the **portly** (stout) lady, I was penitent.

   註解　肥大的 (形容詞)

2034. Many of your helpers are **shiftless** (idle) and slipshod.

   註解　懶惰的 (形容詞)

2035. The **wily** (crafty) boy found a significant concealed note.

   註解　狡猾的 (形容詞)

2036. Your daughters have exquisite eyes and **ruddy** (red) cheeks.

   註解　紅色的 (形容詞)

2037. A compassionate nurse comforted the **dejected** (downhearted) patient.

註解 失望的 (形容詞)

2038. The old gentleman is **infirm** (feeble), but he is still very droll.

註解 虛弱的 (形容詞)

2039. He's a competent sports announcer, but he's **partial** (one-sided).

註解 偏袒的 (形容詞)

2040. The extraordinary news made the people **elated** (joyous).

註解 興奮的 (形容詞)

2041. When he saw the elephant charging, he **froze** (became frightened) in his tracks.

註解 嚇呆 (動詞)

2042. Until recently the sisters of charity wore an unusual **habit** (garb).

註解 衣服，打扮 (名詞)

2043. He has a **level** (well-balanced) head.

註解 健全的 (形容詞)

2044. Heat will **temper** (soften) metal.

註解 鍛鍊，軟化 (動詞)

2045. The rain may **cause** (effect) the river to overflow its banks.

註解 引起 (動詞)

2046. Cut the material on the **bias** (oblique line).

註解 斜線 (名詞)

2047. The tire **tread** (the part of a wheel) made a big hole in my driveway.

註解 輪底 (名詞)

2048. Don't **tread** (walk) on the vegetable garden.

註解 踐踏 (動詞)

2049. The little boy splashed through the **pool** (puddle) of water on the sidewalk.

註解 小水坑 (名詞)

2050. The men will **pool** (form a pool of) their knowledge of missiles to design a new rocket.

註解 共同使用 (動詞)

2051. The **pool** (group of people) of substitute teacher is rater small.

註解 一群人 (名詞)

2052. Minnesota Fats is a famous **pool** (pocket billiards) player.

　　註解　撞球戲 (名詞)

2053. Is she going to **follow** (accept) the profession of her father?

　　註解　追隨 (不定詞)

2054. I couldn't **follow** (keep up with) the teacher when she was reading the play.

　　註解　跟上 (動詞)

2055. The recipe called for the **zest** (flavor) of an orange.

　　註解　風味 (名詞)

2056. He had **zest** (gusto) for the finer things in life.

　　註解　愛好 (名詞)

2057. **Obedient** (Tractable) citizens comply with the law.

　　註解　服從的 (形容詞)

2058. The **native** (innate) habitat of the koala bear is Australia.

　　註解　固有的 (形容詞)

2059. The literature class we read a **legend** (fable).

　　註解　傳奇 (名詞)

2060. The actor's **fame** (notoriety) spread rapidly.

　　註解　名聲 (名詞)

2061. The secretary will **sort** (assort) the huge stack of papers on her desk.

　　註解　分類整理 (動詞)

2062. What was the robber's **motive** (incentive)?

　　註解　動機 (名詞)

2063. The chairman wanted to **adjourn** (dissolve) the meeting.

　　註解　休會 (不定詞)

2064. To distribute papers or books to a class is to **hand** them **out** (return).

　　註解　發送 (不定詞片語)

2065. He is ordered to **hoist** (exalt) the flag in the morning.

　　註解　升起 (不定詞)

2066. John's ideas about how to solve the problem were so **convincing** (cogent) that I had to agree with him.

　　註解　使人信服的 (名詞)

2067. I **came across** (met by chance) her at the theater yesterday.

　　註解　偶然相遇 (動詞片語)

2068. Mrs. Jones sat by the window **mending** (parching) the hole in her coat.

　註解　修補 (動名詞)

2069. He **sneered** (girded) t me in the presence of the guests.

　註解　嘲笑 (動詞)

2070. If you keep bread too long, it becomes **musty** (stale).

　註解　發霉的 (形容詞)

2071. He **ushered** (guided) me to my seat at once.

　註解　引導 (動詞)

2072. The governor's helicopter **hovered** (flies) over the field for a long time before landing.

　註解　盤旋 (動詞)

2073. When the little boy lost his toy, his **dejection** (depression) was so great that I, too, became sad.

　註解　沮喪 (名詞)

2074. To make someone angry is to **enrage** (aggravate).

　註解　激怒 (不定詞)

2075. The banner of Harward is in **crimson** (deep red).

　註解　深紅色 (名詞)

2076. Old John is poor but **venerable** (respectable).

　註解　令人尊敬的 (形容詞)

2077. People were ill seriously because of a **famine** (great hunger).

　註解　飢餓 (名詞)

2078. Our classmates **hail** (give a welcoming cry) to the new comers.

　註解　歡呼 (動詞)

2079. A farmer can't grow much on **barren** (unproductive) land.

　註解　不毛的 (形容詞)

2080. A man's body dies, but his soul may be **perpetual** (continuing forever).

　註解　永恆的 (形容詞)

2081. The girl student **giggle** (laugh foolishly) behind the teacher.

　註解　偷笑 (動詞)

2082. He is **incompetent** (not qualified) to teach English.

　註解　不能勝任的 (形容詞)

2083. I felt **flattered** (praised insincerely) by the letter.

　註解　奉承的 (形容詞)

2084. Students should **heed** (pay attention to) the teacher.

　　註解　專心到 (動詞)

2085. A(n) **associate** (colleague) of mine dropped in yesterday.

　　註解　夥伴 (名詞)

2086. Did he ever **misguide** (act wrongly) on his stage?

　　註解　誤入歧途 (動詞)

2087. Ladies are always interested in a **gem** (precious stone).

　　註解　珠寶 (名詞)

2088. Be careful. It is **brittle** (fragile).

　　註解　易碎的 (形容詞)

2089. What does Cynthia **fret** (worry) about?

　　註解　焦慮 (動詞)

2090. You should **ponder** (consider carefully) the matter before deciding.

　　註解　深思 (動詞)

2091. Mark **offered** (volunteered) to show the new students around the campus.

　　註解　自願 (動詞)

2092. That is an interesting **apparatus** (device).

　　註解　儀器，策略 (名詞)

2093. A **chasm** (gape) appeared after the earthquake.

　　註解　裂縫 (名詞)

2094. My telephone has rung so often today that it is becoming a **nuisance** (noise).

　　註解　討厭的事，噪音 (名詞)

2095. They **sever** (separate) friendship on account of some misunderstanding.

　　註解　切斷 (動詞)

2096. The man was afraid to eat the apple because it looked **corrupt** (rotten).

　　註解　腐爛的 (形容詞)

2097. We saw a **swarm** (group) of flies on the table.

　　註解　一群 (名詞)

2098. His wealth **diminished** (dwindled into nothingness).

　　註解　消失 (動詞)

2099. When Martha dropped the plate, it **shattered** (smashed).

　　註解　粉碎 (動詞)

2100. We tried to **haul** (pull) timber to the back yard.

　　註解　拖拉 (不定詞)

2101. They **nag** (find fault) with me continuously.

　　註解　挑剔 (動詞)

2102. The teacher **rebuked** (reproached) the students strongly for their laziness.

　　註解　責備 (動詞)

2103. One should always say a thing **prudently** (wisely).

　　註解　謹慎地 (副詞)

2104. He tried to **swerve** (turn aside) the car in order not to hit the kid.

　　註解　轉向 (不定詞)

2105. A **valiant** (gallant) soldier was maimed last night.

　　註解　勇敢的 (形容詞)

2106. He **alleged** (claimed) that he was right.

　　註解　主張 (動詞)

2107. The scientist spent months for **an elaborate** (a complicated) machine.

　　註解　複雜的 (形容詞)

2108. Soldiers have to endure the **discomfort** (inconvenience) during a war.

　　註解　困苦 (名詞)

2109. Never **devour** (eat quickly and hungrily) in front of people.

　　註解　狼吞虎嚥 (動詞)

2110. All the people got surprised greatly by this **abrupt** (sudden) decision.

　　註解　突然的 (形容詞)

2111. Many of the boxes were incorrectly **identified** (labeled).

　　註解　認證 (動詞，被動式)

2112. The tiny part was difficult to **extricate** (remove).

　　註解　脫困，移除 (不定詞)

2113. She hit the chair and **splashed** (spilled) the coffee.

　　註解　濺出 (動詞)

2114. All day we could hear the bees **buzzing** (humming) around the roses in our garden.

　　註解　嗡嗡響 (動名詞)

2115. A silly or foolish remark is said to be **fatuous** (inane).

　　註解　愚昧的 (形容詞)

2116. When darkness came, the police ended their **futile** (useless) search for the lost child.

　　註解　無益的 (形容詞)

2117. The speaker is giving a **luminous** (bright) explanation to us.

　　註解　明晰的 (形容詞)

2118. Did you **designate** (specify) any particular time for us to call?

　　註解　指定 (動詞)

2119. The old house was **infested** (overrun) with rats and insects.

　　註解　騷擾 (動詞，被動式)

2120. Boys have a stronger **tendency** (trend) to fight than girls.

　　註解　傾向 (名詞)

2121. Nelson's voice was so **husky** (hoarse) that he could hardly speak.

　　註解　沙啞的 (名詞)

2122. If something can be easily seen, we say that it is **eminent** (conspicuous).

　　註解　明顯的 (形容詞)

2123. Many kinds of animals are now **extinct** (expired).

　　註解　滅絕的 (形容詞)

2124. Sometimes, his five-year-old son's saying is **quaint** (pleasingly odd).

　　註解　奇怪的 (形容詞)

2125. The club members voted to **nullify** (invalidate) the ban on smoking.

　　註解　取消 (不定詞)

2126. To my knowledge, he is a **shrewd** (keen) business man.

　　註解　精明的 (形容詞)

2127. The stream by the hill looked very **placid** (peaceful).

　　註解　平靜的 (形容詞)

2128. Dan **detests** (dislike very strongly) sport games.

　　註解　痛恨 (動詞)

2129. We **detected** (discovered) a thief in the act of breaking into our house.

　　註解　發現 (動詞)

2130. Don't eat anything **pernicious** (causing great harm) to keep yourself healthy.

　　註解　有害的 (形容詞)

2131. Professor Wilson **declined** (refused) to comment on the current political situation.

   註解　拒絕 (動詞)

2132. The city officials called for an immediate **scrutiny** (investigation) to determine the causes of the accident.

   註解　詳查 (名詞)

2133. A **recluse** (hermit) lives by himself far from other people.

   註解　隱士 (名詞)

2134. She felt sad for a while, but, fortunately, the feeling was **transitory** (momentary).

   註解　短暫的 (形容詞)

2135. Because Joe knew that there were mistakes in his paper, he asked his father not to **edit** (compile) it.

   註解　編輯 (不定詞)

2136. They were not rich people, but their **hilarity** (blitheness) helped them to save quite a lot of money.

   註解　歡樂 (名詞)

2137. He is in the full **vigor** (energy) of manhood.

   註解　活力 (名詞)

2138. That picture still does not hang straight; **tilt** (tip) it just a little to the right.

   註解　傾斜 (動詞)

2139. A (n) **extensive** (far-reaching) inquiries is going on in the court.

   註解　廣泛的 (形容詞)

2140. Wanda thinks Mr. Franks is a **bully** (overbearing person) because he shouted at her and threw stones at her dog.

   註解　惡棍 (名詞)

2141. I didn't stop at John's house because he had visitors, and I didn't want to **intrude** (interlope).

   註解　打擾 (不定詞)

2142. You will be sent to the prison, if you **defy** (oppose) the law.

   註解　違反 (動詞)

2143. His foot was badly **mangled** (mutilate) in the accident.

   註解　撕裂 (動詞，被動式)

2144. There is a **lull** (pause) of the rain, she returns home immediately.

> 註解　停息 (名詞)

2145. We'd better wait inside until the storm **subsides** (mollifies).

> 註解　消退 (動詞)

2146. The tired old man **stumbled** (faltered) alone in the street.

> 註解　蹣跚的走 (動詞)

2147. Mrs. Brown bought the other table instead of this one, which has a **blemish** (smudge) here in the corner.

> 註解　污點 (名詞)

2148. **Wading** (Fording) across a stream, he got the shoes completely wet.

> 註解　跋涉 (動名詞)

2149. The troops must **recoil** (move back) quickly.

> 註解　撤退 (動詞)

2150. They have **fled** (run away) from that city.

> 註解　逃跑 (動詞，完成式)

2151. We **ascribe** (attribute) victory and glory to God.

> 註解　歸於 (動詞)

2152. The president **concurred in** (agreed with) the recommendations of his secretary of state.

> 註解　同意 (動詞片語)

2153. The architect **looked over** (inspected) the blueprints.

> 註解　檢查 (動詞片語)

2154. You have the **option of** (choice of) saying yes or no.

> 註解　選擇 (名詞片語)

2155. The reforms were introduced **gradually** (little by little).

> 註解　漸漸地 (副詞)

2156. The clerk must know which order **takes priority** (is fielded first).

> 註解　優先處理 (動詞片語)

2157. Because lack of space, we must **restrict** (limit) the member of people to fifty.

> 註解　限制 (動詞)

2158. The students promised to **persist in** (continue) their efforts to force the dean's resignation.

> 註解　堅持 (不定詞片語)

2159. The politician successfully **sidestepped** (avoided) many questions put to him by the reports.

> 註解　規避 (動詞)

2160. During that **unstable** (troubled) period, the government could not accomplish much.

> 註解　不安定的 (形容詞)

2161. Production of the chemical was **halted** (terminated) when it was found to cause illnesses in laboratory animals.

> 註解　停止 (動詞，被動式)

2162. Mary was **fled up** (disgusted).

> 註解　嫌惡 (動詞片語，被動式)

2163. We are testing it now **for load tolerance** (to see how much weight it can carry).

> 註解　裝載量 (介詞片語)

2164. The child ate the candy **greedily** (hungrily).

> 註解　貪吃地 (副詞)

2165. They voted to **eliminate** (get rid of) the office of second vice-president.

> 註解　取消 (不定詞)

2166. The professor is **suggesting** (implying) that his colleague is wrong.

> 註解　暗示 (動詞，進行式)

2167. The most important parts of the collection are **inaccessible** (not available) to scholars.

> 註解　不能利用的 (形容詞)

2168. **Eventually** (Ultimately), they plan to buy a house.

> 註解　最後地 (副詞)

2169. Her presentation of the speech was **facile** (effortless).

> 註解　不費功夫的 (形容詞)

2170. Some **residual** (remaining) problems were very difficult to resolve.

> 註解　剩餘的 (形容詞)

2171. Congress emerged from its conflict with the President with its authority **intact** (unimpaired).

> 註解　完整的 (形容詞)

2172. Mary **is potentially** (can become) the best athlete in the group.

> 註解　潛能地 (副詞，但 is 是動詞)

2173. Since they found new breeding grounds, the once scarce birds are **thriving** (flourishing).

　　　　註解　興盛的 (形容詞片語)

2174. James was **oblivious of** (unaware of) the noise.

　　　　註解　不知道的 (形容詞片語)

2175. **Agility** (Nimbleness) is extremely important for a gymnast.

　　　　註解　敏捷 (名詞)

2176. The potatoes were **stored** (kept) in the warehouse.

　　　　註解　保存 (動詞，被動式)

2177. It proved to be a **fruitful** (productive) meeting.

　　　　註解　豐富的 (形容詞)

2178. John had better hurry if he is to make the **deadline** (final date) for sending in his final papers.

　　　　註解　期限 (名詞)

2179. In those years America changed from **agrarian** (farming) economy to industrial economy.

　　　　註解　農業的 (形容詞)

2180. The relations between these two countries have never been more **cordial** (fervent).

　　　　註解　眞誠的 (形容詞)

2181. The lecturer concluded his speech with a concise **summary** (brief outline).

　　　　註解　摘要 (名詞)

2182. The **miserly** (stingy) millionaire refused to part with any of his money.

　　　　註解　吝嗇的 (形容詞)

2183. Although Sam had seen the accident, he was **reluctant** (unwilling) to act as a witness.

　　　　註解　不願意的 (形容詞)

2184. The punishment was not **commensurate with** (proportional with) the seriousness of the crime.

　　　　註解　相稱的 (形容詞片語)

2185. Unless something is done to anger them, camels are usually quite **docile** (obedient).

　　　　註解　溫順的 (形容詞)

2186. Joan's **prediction** (prophecy) that there would be an earthquake dismayed her friends.

    註解　預感 (名詞)

2187. The old couple was **taken in** (deceived) by the young person's lies about him home life.

    註解　欺騙 (動詞片語，被動式)

2188. They refused to **intervene in** (intercede in) the quarrel.

    註解　介入 (不定詞片語)

2189. The physicist was **perplexed** (confused) by the problem.

    註解　迷惑 (動詞，被動式)

2190. His report was organized **chronologically** (according to a time sequence).

    註解　依年代順序地 (副詞)

2191. Having always lived in an **isolated** (remote) area, Tom had never seen a train.

    註解　偏遠的 (形容詞)

2192. The outcome was a result of a series of **random** (unplanned) decisions.

    註解　隨便的 (形容詞)

2193. For the long-distance runner **pace** (timing) is essential.

    註解　步伐 (名詞)

2194. **The bulk** (Most) of the herd had to be destroyed because of disease.

    註解　大部分 (名詞)

2195. John **winced** (shrank back) when his superior yelled at him.

    註解　畏縮 (動詞)

2196. **In retrospect** (Looking back), I think she made the right decision.

    註解　回頭看 (介詞片語)

2197. Although she generally has a broad outlook, Sally can be **narrow-minded** (intolerant) at time.

    註解　心胸狹窄的 (形容詞)

2198. Many people suggest that a **bleak** (desolate) landscape is the most characteristic feature of his paintings.

    註解　荒涼的 (形容詞)

2199. The loss of his inheritance was **a setback to** (a check to the progress of) the artist's career.

    註解　挫折 (名詞片語)

2200. Johns painted the mural **piecemeal** (in stages).

> **註解** 一件件的 (形容詞)

2201. That river certainly **meanders** (winds) all over the countryside.

> **註解** 彎彎曲曲的流 (動詞)

2202. It is theorized that the universe is **expanding** (getting larger) at a rate of fifty miles per second per million light years.

> **註解** 擴大的 (形容詞)

2203. Although he is recognized as one of the most brilliant scientists in his field, Professor white cannot seem to **make his ideas** understood (get his ideas across) in class.

> **註解** 說明白 (不定詞片語)

2204. The **fort** (garrison) now known as Fort Mchenry was built prior to the War of 1812 to guard Baltimore harbor.

> **註解** 保壘 (名詞)

2205. **Unorganized** (Haphazard) guessing will probably not raise a test score as significantly as choosing one letter as a "guess answer" for the entire examination.

> **註解** 隨便的 (形容詞)

2206. Thomas Edison's office was always **disorganized** (cluttered) with books and papers.

> **註解** 雜亂的 (形容詞)

2207. As soon as the board of elections **promulgates** (officially declares) the list of candidates, a ballot is prepared.

> **註解** 公佈 (動詞)

2208. Veterinarians usually give dogs an anesthetic so that they don't **cry out in pain** (yelp).

> **註解** 亂吠 (動詞片語)

2209. If one aids and abets a criminal, he is also considered **guilty of** the crime (culpability).

> **註解** 犯罪 (名詞片語)

2210. The graduate committee must be **in full accord in** (unanimous) their approval of a dissertation.

> **註解** 全體一致的 (介詞片語)

2211. The thief was apprehended, but his **accomplice** (person who helped him) had disappeared.

　　　註解　同謀者 (名詞)

2212. Sometimes items are put on sale because they have **imperfections** (defects) on them.

　　　註解　瑕疵 (名詞)

2213. Many doctors are still general practitioners, but the **tendency** (trend) is toward specialization in medicine.

　　　註解　趨勢 (名詞)

2214. Electrical energy may be divided into two components **specified** (designated) as positive and negative.

　　　註解　分類 (動詞，被動式)

2215. Historical records reveal that Jefferson **reiterated** (repeated) his ideas about a meritocracy.

　　　註解　反覆地說 (動詞)

2216. Because of a long drought, Midwestern farmers are **doubtful** (dubious) about the prospect of a good yield.

　　　註解　懷疑的 (形容詞)

2217. **Proximity to** (Nearness to) the court house makes an office building more valuable.

　　　註解　接近 (名詞片語)

2218. The rock music made popular by the Beathes has been **modified** (changed) over the past two decades.

　　　註解　變更 (動詞，完成被動式)

2219. Architects must consider whether their designs are likely to be **very wet** (drenched) suddenly downpours.

　　　註解　溼透的 (形容詞片語)

2220. Mail service will be **suspended** (curtailed) during the postal workers' strike.

　　　註解　停止 (動詞，被動式)

2221. A compound **break** (fracture) is more serious than a simple one because there is more opportunity for loss of blood and infection.

　　　註解　挫傷 (名詞)

2222. Even though the evidence is overwhelming, if one juror is still **skeptical** (not convinced), the case must be retried.

> 註解　懷疑的 (形容詞)

2223. In Benjamin Franklin's almanac, he warns against making **hasty** (quick) decisions.

> 註解　急忙的 (形容詞)

2224. **Prior to** (Before) his appointment as secretary of state, Henry Kissinger was a professor of government and international affairs at Harvard.

> 註解　以前的 (形容詞，但 Before 是介詞)

2225. Arson is suspected in a fire that **razed** (destroyed) the Grand Hotel.

> 註解　摧毀 (動詞)

2226. When one is unfamiliar with the customs, it is easy to make **a blunder** (a mistake).

> 註解　錯誤 (名詞)

2227. A good student is eager to learn and does need to be **warned** (admonished) for being absent too much.

> 註解　勸告 (不定詞，被動式)

2228. Psychologists encourage their patients not to get upset about **trivial** (unimportant) matters.

> 註解　不重要的 (形容詞)

2229. Trees that **block** (obstruct) the view of oncoming traffic should be cut down.

> 註解　阻礙 (動詞)

2230. In the play The Devil and Daniel Webster, the **retorts** (replies) attributed to Webster may be more fiction than history.

> 註解　反應 (名詞)

2231. People who live in the country enjoy a **rustic** (simple) life style.

> 註解　樸實的 (形容詞)

2232. In the famous nursery rhyme about Jack and Jill, Jill **tumbled** (fell) down the hill after Jack.

> 註解　跌倒 (動詞)

2233. Professor Baker is **a coworker** (a colleague) of Professor Ayers.

> 註解　同事 (名詞)

2234. When Pope John Paul visited Latin America, he often **signaled for** (beckoned) the children to come to him.

> 註解　招手 (動詞片語)

2235. In his biography, Thomas Hardy is described as very **industrious** (diligent) writer.

> 註解　勤勉的 (形容詞)

2236. In several states, the people may recommend a law to the legislature by signing a **request** (petition).

> 註解　請願書 (名詞)

2237. It is not a good business policy to **sleazy** (cheap) materials.

> 註解　質料不佳的 (形容詞)

2238. It is much easier to talk about social change than it is to **make it happen** (bring is about).

> 註解　突然發生 (不定詞片語)

2239. Sometimes, while living in a foreign country, one **craves** (desires) a special dish from home.

> 註解　渴望 (動詞)

2240. **Variations** (Changes) in the color of sea water from blue to green seem to be caused by high or low concentrations of salt.

> 註解　變化 (名詞)

2241. **Lifting the shoulders** (Shrugging) is a gesture that indicates lack of interest.

> 註解　聳聳肩 (動名詞片語)

2242. In frogs and toads, the tongue is fixed to the front of the mouth in order to facilitate **projecting** (protruding) it at some distance, greatly aiding in the capture of insects.

> 註解　吐出 (動名詞)

2243. The constitution guarantees that private homes will not be searched without a **warrant** (written authorization).

> 註解　搜索狀 (名詞)

2244. Lindbergh's first nonstop flight across the Atlantic Ocean was **an act** (a feat) of great daring and courage.

> 註解　功績 (名詞)

2245. What may be considered courteous in one culture may be interpreted as **arrogant** (surly) in another.

註解 傲慢的 (形容詞)

2246. Because tornadoes are more **prevalent** (widespread) in the middle states, the area from Minesota to Texas is called Tornado Alley.

註解 普遍的 (形容詞)

2247. Some **celestial bodies** (meteors) will leave luminous trails upon entering the earth's atmosphere.

註解 隕石 (名詞)

2248. A **thrifty** (careful) buyer purchases fruits and vegetables in season.

註解 節儉的 (形容詞)

2249. **Vendors** (Everyone engaged in selling) must have a license.

註解 販賣者 (名詞，同 Venders)

2250. The system of Daylight Savings Time seems very **silly** (foolish) until one understands why it is done.

註解 愚笨的 (形容詞)

2251. A **clever** (shrewd) politician will take advantage of every speaking engagement to campaign for the next election.

註解 精明的 (形容詞)

2252. One must **live in** (reside in) the Unites States five years in order to apply for citizenship.

註解 居住 (動詞片語)

2253. In the play Who's Afraid of Virginia Woolf? A woman and her husband spend most of their time **quarreling** (bickering).

註解 爭吵 (動名詞)

2254. Madame Curie was completely **engrossed** (absorbed) in her work.

註解 全神貫注的 (形容詞)

2255. When students do not have time to read a novel before class, they read **an outline of the plot** (a synopsis) instead.

註解 概要 (名詞片語)

2256. A balance of international payment refers to the net result of the business which a nation **carries on** (transacts) with other nations in a given period.

註解 交易 (動詞片語)

2257. In order to be issued a passport, one must either present legal documents or call a witness to **give evidence** (testify) concerning one's identity.

> 註解　證明 (不定詞片語)

2258. Regan seemed **sure** (confident) that he would win the election.

> 註解　自信的 (形容詞)

2259. The author of a book, a musical composition, or an artistic work may choose to honor someone by putting his or her name in the front of it, thereby **giving** (dedicating) it.

> 註解　奉獻 (動名詞)

2260. **Strive** (Make efforts) for excellence.

> 註解　努力 (動詞)

2261. The Miami Port Authorities have **seized** (confiscated) over a million dollars worth of illegal drugs.

> 註解　沒收 (動詞，完成式)

2262. The representatives of the company seemed very **callous** (insensitive) concerning the conditions of the workers.

> 註解　無情的 (形容詞)

2263. Home buyers are proceeding **cautiously** (warily) because of the high interest rates.

> 註解　小心地 (副詞)

2264. Even though the critics are not enthusiastic, some of the plays off Broadway are very **funny** (hilarious).

> 註解　熱鬧的 (形容詞)

2265. Tiny Tim, a character in AChristmas Carol, was a happy little boy in spite of disability that caused him **to favor one leg** (limp).

> 註解　跛行 (不定詞片詞)

2266. The value of **an old item** (an antique) increases with time.

> 註解　古董 (名詞片語)

2267. Dali's paintings can inspire a **pensive** (thoughtful) mood.

> 註解　憂鬱的 (形容詞)

2268. The **ultimate** (final) cause of the Civil War was the bombardment of Fort Sumter.

> 註解　最終的 (形容詞)

2269. Due to the efforts of conservationists and environmentalists, few people are **unaware of** (ignorant of) the problems of endangered species.

> 註解　無知的 (形容詞片語)

2270. Ethnocentrism prevents us from **putting up with** (tolerating) all of the customs we encounter in another culture.

> 註解　忍受 (動名詞片語)

2271. Pipes may be painted to keep them from getting **oxidized** (rusty).

> 註解　生鏽的 (形容詞)

2272. Frontier settlements had to **depend on** (trust) the cavalry.

> 註解　依靠 (不定詞片語)

2273. The copperhead, a snake that strikes without warning, is considered much more **dangerous** (treacherous) than the rattlesnake.

> 註解　危險的 (形容詞)

2274. Phosphorus is used in paints for highway signs and marks because it is **bright** (luminous) at night.

> 註解　發亮的 (形容詞)

2275. Shelley's famous poem "To a Skylark" praises the bird for its **carefree** (blithe) spirit.

> 註解　快樂的 (形容詞)

2276. For your safety and the safety of others, always **heed** (pay attention to) traffic signals.

> 註解　注意 (動詞)

2277. **Interfering** (Tampering) with someone's mail is a serious crime in the U.S.A.

> 註解　干涉 (動名詞)

2278. It is very discourteous to **intrude** (be in the way) during someone's conversation.

> 註解　打擾 (不定詞)

2279. The **remnants** (small pieces) of the Roman Empire can be found in many countries in Asia, Europe, and Africa.

> 註解　殘餘物 (名詞)

2280. Chemicals are used to **retard** (stunt) the growth of ornamental trees.

> 註解　阻礙(不定詞)

2281. The development of general anesthetics has allowed doctors to operate without the **pain** (anguish) once associated with surgery.

> 註解　病痛 (名詞)

2282. Neon is an element which does not combine readily with any other element; because of this property, it is called an **inactive** (inert) element.

> 註解　惰性的 (形容詞)

2283. **Finances** (Assets) can consist of a combination of stocks, bonds, and properties.

> 註解　資產 (名詞)

2284. In some states drivers are fined $100 for **careless** (reckless) driving.

> 註解　疏失的 (形容詞)

2285. The landscape can change **abruptly** (quickly) after a rainstorm in the desert Southwest.

> 註解　突然地 (副詞)

2286. Some stretches of Florida **resemble** (look like) West Africa.

> 註解　相似的 (形容詞)

2287. **Severe snowstorms** (Blizzards) cause power failures in the Northeast every winter.

> 註解　暴風雪 (名詞)

2288. Attending a church, temple, or mosque is one way to make **agreeable** (congenial) friends.

> <註解 意氣相投的 (形容詞)

2289. An understudy performs when the lead singer's voice becomes **hoarse** (rough).

> 註解　沙啞的 (形容詞)

2290. In case of poisoning, immediately give large quantities of soapy or salty water in order to **induce** (cause) vomiting.

> 註解　引起 (不定詞)

2291. Because of the extreme pressure underwater, divers are often **sluggish** (slow).

> 註解　緩慢的 (形容詞)

2292. The Supreme Court has a reputation for being **just** (impartial).

> 註解　公正的 (形容詞)

2293. The **law officers** (marshals) in many early Western settlements had to maintain order by means of their guns.

　註解　警官 (名詞)

2294. Because the Amtrak system is so old, the trains always start **suddenly** (with a jerk).

　註解　突然地 (副詞)

2295. Rain **lessens** (abates) in the fall throughout most of the Appalachian Mountain region.

　註解　減少 (動詞)

2296. Feeling **irritable** (grouchy) may be a side effect of too much medication.

　註解　不悅的 (形容詞)

2297. Travel agents will **confirm** (verify) your reservations for you free.

　註解　確認 (動詞)

2298. To **look quickly through** (skim) a book is an important study skill.

　註解　掠過閱讀 (不定詞片語)

2299. By law, when one makes a large purchase he must have an **adequate** (ample) opportunity to change his mind.

　註解　充分的 (形容詞)

2300. In order to enjoy fine wine, one should **drink** (sip) it slowly, a little at a time.

　註解　啜飲 (動詞)

2301. Several members of the royal family have been held **prisoner** (captive) in the Tower of London.

　註解　俘虜 (名詞)

2302. A series of **columns** (pillars) supporting a large porch is typical of the architecture of pre-Civil War mansions in the South.

　註解　柱子 (名詞)

2303. J.P. Morgan had a reputation for being a **prudent** (careful) businessman.

　註解　謹慎的 (形容詞)

2304. Einstein's theory of relativity seemed **incredible** (unbelievable) at the time that he first introduced it.

　註解　令人難以相信的 (形容詞)

2305. A cut in the budget put 10 percent of the state employee's jobs in **jeopardy** (danger).

   註解   危險 (名詞)

2306. Unless the **agreement** (concord) contains a provision for a United Nations peace-keeping force to patrol the lords, the General Assemlly is not likely to ratify it.

   註解   一致 (名詞)

2307. A marching band often performs during the **time** (interval) between the two halves of a football game.

   註解   中間的時間 (名詞)

2308. Preservatives are added to bread to keep it from getting **stale** (old).

   註解   不新鮮的 (形容詞)

2309. Discretionary funds are included in most budgets to cover expenses that the contractor might **run into** (meet unexpectedly) during the work.

   註解   偶遇 (動詞片語)

2310. Congress was **hesitant** (reluctant) to repeal the Prohibition Act.

   註解   猶豫的 (形容詞)

2311. When baseball players became **impatient** (exasperated) with their contracts, they went on strike, causing most of the 1981 season to be lost.

   註解   不耐煩的 (形容詞)

2312. When Joan of Arc described her vision, her voice did not **hesitate** (falter).

   註解   心生動搖 (動詞)

2313. Athletes learn to **conceal** (disguise) their disappointment when they lose.

   註解   隱藏 (不定詞)

2314. That a driver **swerves** (turns sharply) in order to avoid an accident can be proven by examining the marks on the pavement.

   註解   轉向 (動詞)

2315. The successful use of antitoxins and serums has virtually **eradicated** (removed) the threat of malaria, yellow fever, and other insect-borne diseases.

   註解   根除 (動詞，完成式)

2316. The president is often awakened by a **clamorous** (noisy) crowd which assembles on the White House lawn to protest his policies.

   註解   吵鬧的 (形容詞)

2317. In the past, energy sources were thought to be **boundless** (without limits).

   註解　無限的 (形容詞)

2318. Although monkeys occasionally **menace** (threaten) their enemies, they are usually not dangerous unless they are provoked.

   註解　威脅 (動詞)

2319. Even as a child Thomas Edison had a very **inquisitive** (curious) mind, at the age of three he performed his first experiment.

   註解　好奇的 (形容詞)

2320. The audience **applauded** (clapped) enthusiastically after the performance at the Grand Old Opera.

   註解　鼓掌 (動詞)

2321. Some of the gangs that terrorized Chicago in the 1920s did not have the **propriety** (decency) to keep their activities off the streets.

   註解　適當行為 (名詞)

2322. It will be necessary for the doctor to **dilate** (widen) the pupils of your eyes with some drops in order to examine them.

   註解　擴大 (不定詞)

2323. Mark Anthony's **eulogy** (praise) of Caesar at his funeral is memorably recorded in a play by Shakespeare.

   註解　讚美 (名詞)

2324. Flatboats **ferry** (transport) cars on the Great Lakes between the United States and Canada.

   註解　渡過湖或河 (動詞)

2325. News commentator, Eric Sevareid, had to yell to be heard above the **hubbub** (noise and confusion).

   註解　喧嘩 (名詞)

2326. Legislators are considering whether the drug laws for possession of marijuana are too **severe** (harsh).

   註解　嚴厲的 (形容詞)

2327. **Cruel** (Brutal) treatment of inmates instigated a riot in one of the Indiana prisons.

   註解　殘酷的 (形容詞)

2328. The Civil War in 1863 **severed** (cut) the United States into nations—a southern Confederacy and a Northern Union.

    註解 切斷 (動詞)

2329. Milk is **purified** (cleansed) by heating it at 60°C for thirty minutes.

    註解 清淨 (動詞，被動式)

2330. Drink only **tepid** (slightly warm) liquids.

    註解 微溫的 (形容詞)

2331. It is difficult to **discern** (determine) the sample that is on the slide unless the microscope is adjusted.

    註解 辨別 (不定詞)

2332. The Revolutionary forces had to **muster up** (gather) enough men to oppose the British army.

    註解 集合 (不定詞片語)

2333. A laser beam is used to **penetrate** (pass through) even the hardest substances.

    註解 穿透 (不定詞)

2334. The National Institute of Mental Health is conducting **far-reaching** (extensive) research to determine the psychological effects of using drugs.

    註解 廣泛的 (形容詞)

2335. The box fell off his desk and hit the floor with a **thump** (dull noise).

    註解 砰撞聲 (名詞)

2336. The TOEFL examination will begin **precisely** (exactly) at eight-thirty.

    註解 正確地 (副詞)

2337. John Dewey **loathed** (hated) the idea that children should not participate in activities as part of their educational experience.

    註解 不願意 (動詞)

2338. The Boy Scouts usually sell **apple juice** (cider) in the fall in order to earn money for their activities.

    註解 蘋果汁 (名詞)

2339. Ralph Nader always **speaks out** (declares his opinion) about everything.

    註解 說明 (動詞片語)

2340. In American football, the coach may **shout** (bellow) to the captain to call time out.

    註解 吼叫 (動詞)

2341. Flu shots are given every fall as a **precaution** (preventive measure) against an epidemic the following winter.

   註解　預防 (名詞)

2342. The other members of the cabinet **made fun of** (derided) the Secretary of Interior when he purchased Alaska because, at the time, it was not considered valuable.

   註解　嘲笑 (動詞片語)

2343. The **pact** (treaty) has been in effect for twenty years.

   註解　協定 (名詞)

2344. Since none of the polls had predicted the winner, everyone was **astounded** (surprised) by the results of the election.

   註解　驚奇的 (形容詞)

2345. If the teams were not so evenly matched, it would be easier to **predict** (foretell) the outcome of the Superbowl.

   註解　預測 (不定詞)

2346. A monument was erected in memory of those who died in the **cataclysm** (disaster) at Johnstown, Pennsylvania.

   註解　災難 (名詞)

2347. When a hurricane is **about to occur** (imminent), the National Weather Bureau issues a warning.

   註解　即將發生的 (介詞片語)

2348. Relaxation therapy teaches one not to **fret over** (worry about) small problems.

   註解　煩惱 (不定詞片語)

2349. The **perpetual** (constant) motion of the earth as it turns on its axis creates the change of seasons.

   註解　不中斷的 (形容詞)

2350. Keep two pencils **handy** (near) while taking the examination.

   註解　方便的，手邊的 (形容詞)

2351. Martin Luther King **detested** (abhorred) injustice.

   註解　痛恨 (動詞)

2352. It is impossible for parents to **shield** (protect) their children from every danger.

   註解　保護 (不定詞)

2353. His winning the award was the highest **attainment** (achievement) of his career.

   > 註解 成就 (名詞)

2354. Both a person's heredity and his **surroundings** (environment) help to shape his character.

   > 註解 環境 (名詞)

2355. When the eye of the hurricane passed over, there was a **lull** (calm interval) in the storm.

   > 註解 平靜 (名詞)

2356. That student is discourteous; he **grumbles** (complains) no matter how one tries to please him.

   > 註解 埋怨 (動詞)

2357. The old woman is too **feeble** (weak) to cross the street without her nephew's help.

   > 註解 衰弱的 (形容詞)

2358. Your mood seems very **meditative** (thoughtful) this evening.

   > 註解 沉思的 (形容詞)

2359. The **tunnel** (underground passageway) was so dark and clammy that we became frightened.

   > 註解 隧道 (名詞)

2360. His natural intelligence and his experience enabled him to **cope** (deal) with the problem.

   > 註解 應付 (不定詞)

2361. The officer **compelled** (forced) the suspect to wait at the scene of the crime.

   > 註解 強迫 (動詞)

2362. Do not leave the iron on that delicate fabric or the heat will **scorch** (discolor) it.

   > 註解 燒焦，褪色 (動詞)

2363. There is no **alterative** (other choice); the president must approve the bill if Congress passes it.

   > 註解 改變 (名詞)

2364. My supply confidence slowly **dwindles** (diminishes) as the deadline approaches.

> 註解　減少 (動詞)

2365. The theory that business could operate totally without the aid of government has proved to be an erroneous **belief** (illusion).

> 註解　幻想 (名詞)

2366. The young man was so **bashful** (shy) that he did not speak to the pretty girl.

> 註解　害羞的 (形容詞)

2367. The new contact lenses made the woman **blink** (open and close) her eyes much more than usual.

> 註解　眨眼 (動詞，使役動詞 made 之後加原型動詞)

2368. It is **futile** (useless) to argue with him once he has made up his mind.

> 註解　無用的 (形容詞)

2369. I knew my father would **discipline** (punish) me for my actions.

> 註解　教訓 (動詞)

2370. Can this be a **duplicate** (copy) of the document?

> 註解　影印本 (名詞)

2371. Many businesses provide a kind of **retirement benefit** (pension) which is paid until the death of the former employee.

> 註解　養老金 (名詞片語)

2372. He will **abide by** (stick to) his promise if he gives it.

> 註解　堅持 (動詞片語)

2373. The man walked **briskly** (quickly) to keep warm on the very cold night.

> 註解　匆匆地 (副詞)

2374. He **hurled** (threw) the statue to the floor with such force that it shattered.

> 註解　投擲 (動詞)

2375. Samuel Morse's painting ability has been **obscured** (hidden) by his other.

> 註解　不清楚 (動詞，完成被動式)

2376. The gunfire was **sporadic** (intermittent).

> 註解　斷斷續續的 (形容詞)

2377. The man **neglected** (failed) to file his income tax and therefore had to pay a fine.

> 註解　疏忽 (動詞)

2378. The rock was **poised** (balanced) on the edge of the cliff.

> 註解　平衡的 (形容詞)

2379. Michael was such a **shrewd** (clever) businessperson that never lost money in any transaction.

> 註解　聰明的 (形容詞)

2380. He is the most **intrepid** (fearless) explorer in the present century.

> 註解　勇猛的 (形容詞)

2381. Th earth is usually represented by a **sphere** (globe).

> 註解　天體，球狀的 (名詞)

2382. The chairman did not **rule out** (reject) the possibility of an agreement.

> 註解　否認 (動詞片語)

2383. The Civil Defense **evacuated** (removed)all inhabitants from the area where the storm was predicted to strike.

> 註解　撤離 (動詞)

2384. There was no **trace** (indication) of poison in the coffee the chemist analyzed.

> 註解　跡象 (名詞)

2385. It is not easy to remain **tranquil** (serene) when events suddenly change your life.

> 註解　平靜的 (形容詞)

2386. He was able to **mend** (repair) the cup and saucer.

> 註解　修補 (不定詞)

2387. **Punctuality** (Being on time) is imperative in your new job.

> 註解　準時 (名詞)

2388. According to its label, that medicine should **take effect** (produce results) in about ten minutes.

> 註解　發生效用 (動詞片語)

2389. The student **revised** (corrected) his paper carefully, following the professor's suggestions.

> 註解　修正 (動詞)

2390. The **intricate** (complicated) directions were difficult to understand.

> 註解　複雜的 (形容詞)

2391. One **symptom** (sign) of the disease is a high fever.

> 註解　徵狀 (名詞)

2392. The girl took a long **hike** (walk) on her first morning at camp.

註解 遠足 (名詞)

2393. He **got nowhere** (accomplished nothing) with his plan to balance the budget.

註解 別無選擇 (動詞片語)

2394. She is always **diplomatic** (tactful) when she deals with angry students.

註解 圓滑的 (形容詞)

2395. We will **wind up** (conclude) out business on Friday and take the weekend off.

註解 結束 (動詞片語)

2396. The little boy had had a long day; he was feeling **drowsy** (sleepy).

註解 愛睏的 (形容詞)

2397. He was greatly **vexed** (annoyed) by the new and unexpected development.

註解 苦惱的 (形容詞)

2398. Before taking such a test, one had better **brush up on** (review) his or her vocabulary.

註解 溫習 (動詞片語)

2399. He ate a **prodigious** (huge) amount of the homemade bread.

註解 很大的 (形容詞)

2400. The professor **dictated** (read) the words to her class, who wrote them down in the phonetic alphabet.

註解 口唸 (動詞，別人聽寫)

2401. The water **trickled** (dripped steadily) over the edge of the basin.

註解 滴流 (動詞)

2402. Since I have been ill, my **appetite** (desire for food) has diminished.

註解 食慾 (名詞)

2403. The clerk had been **insolent** (rude) to his superior once too often; now he was without a job.

註解 粗魯的 (形容詞)

2404. It is **ridiculous** (absurd) to become angry about such an insignificant matter.

註解 可笑的 (形容詞)

2405. He is **infamous** (notorious) for his dishonesty in business matters.

　　　註解　　無恥的 (形容詞)

2406. His **hobby** (pastime) is collecting stamps from all over the world.

　　　註解　　嗜好 (名詞)

2407. The judge **sentenced** (passed judgment upon) the convicted man.

　　　註解　　判決 (動詞)

2408. He **stayed late** (lingered) to tell his hostess how much he had enjoyed the party.

　　　註解　　遲緩 (動詞片語)

2409. The picture is **tilted** (crooked); please straighten it.

　　　註解　　傾斜的 (形容詞)

2410. The official **hinted at** (indirectly suggested) startling new developments that would soon be made public.

　　　註解　　暗示 (動詞片語)

2411. Gradually, the sound of the music and laughter **died down** (became softer).

　　　註解　　減弱 (動詞片語)

2412. The characters in this novel are **fictitious** (not real people).

　　　註解　　捏造的 (形容詞)

2413. The night was so **foggy** (misty) that the murderer was easily able to escape his pursuers.

　　　註解　　濃霧的 (形容詞)

2414. His employer appeared to be in such an **affable** (agreeable) mood that Tom decided to ask for a raise.

　　　註解　　可親的 (形容詞)

2415. The orchid is an **exotic** (unusual) plant to see blooming in most North American gardens.

　　　註解　　外來的 (形容詞)

2416. The hunter carefully **stalked** (tracked) the deer.

　　　註解　　潛行，追蹤 (動詞)

2417. The climate in the great plains is **arid** (hot and dry).

　　　註解　　乾旱的 (形容詞)

2418. At the battle of Waterloo, Napoleon's forces **retreated** (withdrew).

　　　註解　　撤退 (動詞)

2419. The house finally came to a halt on the very **rim** (edge) of the cliff.
註解 邊緣 (名詞)

2420. The boy felt **disgraced** (ashamed) because he knew that he had been wrong to steal.
註解 恥辱的 (形容詞)

2421. The crowd **swelled** (grew) until the noise made could be heard for miles.
註解 增大 (動詞)

2422. There is a large area of **swamp** (soft, wet land) that will have to be cleared before construction can begin.
註解 沼澤 (名詞)

2423. The speaker **demonstrated** (showed) his knowledge of the subject by his excellent lecture.
註解 表露 (動詞)

2424. To everyone but the expert, the painting's defects were **invisible** (unable to be seen).
註解 無法看見的 (形容詞)

2425. Her husband is very **competent** (proficient); he will repair the roof himself.
註解 能幹的 (形容詞)

2426. Since he had never been in such a situation before, his **apprehension** (fear) was understandable.
註解 憂慮 (名詞)

2427. The flowers will **wither** (dry up) in a few hours.
註解 枯萎 (動詞)

2428. For once, everything in her life seemed to be in **equilibrium** (balance).
註解 平衡 (名詞)

2429. When the bell rang, the chemistry student **jerked** (abruptly pulled) her hand and spilled the acid.
註解 急拉 (動詞)

2430. The child **groped** (searched blindly) for the light switch.
註解 盲目尋找 (動詞)

2431. Mr. Henderson was determined to remain **neutral** (uncommitted).
註解 中立的 (形容詞)

2432. A sealed bottle thrown into the ocean often **floats aimlessly** (drifts) before it reaches land.

> 註解　漂流 (動詞片語)

2433. The indecisive man was **readily** (easily) persuaded to change his mind again.

> 註解　容易地 (副詞)

2434. The world leaders had a **chat** (friendly, unimportant talk) before beginning formal negotiations.

> 註解　閒談 (名詞)

2435. **Subsequent** (Later) events proved the man to be right.

> 註解　後來的 (形容詞)

2436. The war ended when the **armistice** (truce) was signed.

> 註解　休戰 (名詞)

2437. The **stray** (homeless) dog was picked up by the dogcatcher because he had no collar.

> 註解　流浪的 (形容詞)

2438. His face was **flushed** (red) because he had run all the way from the dormitory.

> 註解　紅色的 (形容詞)

2439. He was too old to keep up the **pace** (speed) for more than a few miles.

> 註解　速度 (名詞)

2440. Where did she **acquire** (gain) all her wealth?

> 註解　獲得 (動詞)

2441. He is **dubious** (doubtful) about the success of the plan.

> 註解　懷疑的 (形容詞)

2442. The patient handed the doctor his **fee** (money).

> 註解　費用 (名詞)

2443. The time for **discussing** (talking about) the problem is over; now we must act.

> 註解　討論 (動名詞)

2444. The **initial** (first) step is often the most difficult.

> 註解　開始的 (形容詞)

2445. The candidate's **victory** (triumph) at the polls was overwhelming.

> 註解　勝利 (名詞)

2446. He **resolved** (decided) to act more wisely in the future.

　　註解　決定 (動詞)

2447. All students should **bear in mind** (remember) that these books must be read by mid-semester.

　　註解　記住 (動詞片語)

2448. The driver tried to **avert** (prevent) the accident by bringing the car to a sudden stop.

　　註解　避免 (不定詞)

2449. His **apparel** (clothing)showed him to be a successful man.

　　註解　服裝 (名詞)

2450. The noise was so **faint** (indistinct) that it was impossible to be sure what it was or even where it came from.

　　註解　微弱的 (形容詞)

2451. By taking larger seams, it is a simple matter to **alter** (change)

　　註解　改變 (不定詞)

2452. The jeweler reported that the diamonds were **genuine** (real).

　　註解　眞實的 (形容詞)

2453. The man listened to reports of the approaching hurricane with mounting **anxiety** (uneasiness).

　　註解　憂慮 (名詞)

2454. The warmth of the room made the student **doze** (fall asleep).

　　註解　打瞌睡 (動詞，使役動詞 made 之後加原型動詞)

2455. He agreed to the plan **of his own accord** (voluntarily).

　　註解　自願地 (介詞片語當副詞用)

2456. The clerk had to **break off** (interrupt) the conversation in order to wait on a customer.

　　註解　中斷 (不定詞片語)

2457. It is useless to attempt to **flee** (run away) from every danger; some risks must be taken.

　　註解　逃跑 (不定詞)

2458. I decided to go to the party on the **spur of the moment** (without previous thought).

　　註解　一時的衝動 (名詞片語)

2459. The criminal **insinuated** (suggested indirectly) that he had been roughly treated by the arresting officer.

> 註解 暗指 (動詞片語)

2460. When he heard the news, he was overcome with **grief** (sorrow).

> 註解 悲傷 (名詞)

2461. **Ignoring** (Paying no attention to) something will not make it go away.

> 註解 不留心 (分詞)

2462. The mother **soothed** (comforted) the disappointed child and then promised to take him on a picnic.

> 註解 安慰 (動詞)

2463. The political leader was **revered** (loved) by the people of his country.

> 註解 尊敬 (動詞，被動式)

2464. The winners will be selected **at random** (by chance).

> 註解 隨便地 (副詞片語)

2465. She is a **contemporary** (modern) writer who has received much critical acclaim.

> 註解 現在同時代的 (形容詞)

2466. At first, the incident seemed to be **trivial** (unimportant).

> 註解 不重要的 (形容詞)

2467. During the war, the shipping lanes proved **vulnerable** (susceptible) to attack.

> 註解 易受攻擊的 (形容詞)

2468. The new tax law is **explicit** (definite); that type of certificate is tax-exempt.

> 註解 明確的 (形容詞)

2469. The history professor gave a **synopsis** (summary) of the events leading to World War I.

> 註解 概要 (名詞)

2470. **Pilfering** (Stealing) by company employees costs many business thousands of dollars each year.

> 註解 偷竊 (動名詞)

2471. No **remnants** (traces) of the settlement of Roanoke, Virginia were found by the next group of colonists.

> 註解 造物 (名詞)

2472. The proposed environmental amendment has not been **ratified** (approved) by all fifty states.

> 註解　批准 (動詞，被動完成式)

2473. The charges brought against the government official finally hurt nothing but his **vanity** (pride).

> 註解　虛榮 (名詞)

2474. Zinnia seeds will begin to **germinate** (grow) in seven to ten days.

> 註解　發芽 (不定詞)

2475. The noisy **throng** (crowd) of teenagers jammed the hall to hear the rock concert.

> 註解　群眾 (名詞)

2476. The relativity theory is **basically** (fundamentally) made up of two parts: the restricted and the general relativity theory.

> 註解　基本地 (副詞)

2477. The soldier **rashly** (recklessly) agreed to lead the dangerous expedition.

> 註解　不留心地 (副詞)

2478. Hurricanes often **devastate** (destroy) the coffee crop, Haiti's principal export.

> 註解　破壞 (動詞)

2479. According to investigators, the recent report of a sea monster was a **hoax** (trick).

> 註解　愚弄 (名詞)

2480. The union's **grievance** (complaint) committee met with the school board to protest the teacher's firing.

> 註解　苦境，訴苦 (名詞)

2481. That matter is so **confidential** (secret) that it must not be discussed outside this office.

> 註解　秘密的 (形容詞)

2482. The Seles representatives were asked to **go over** (review) the figures in their reports before the conference.

> 註解　檢視 (不定詞片語)

2483. It is vital to recognize that emotions **trigger** (activator) physiological reactions and vice versa.

> 註解　扳機，反應器 (名詞)

2484. In his statements to the press, the administrator was consistently **equivocal** (ambiguous).

> 註解　意義含糊的 (形容詞)

2485. Argon, an **inert** (inactive) gas, constitutes nearly one percent of the atmosphere.

> 註解　惰性的 (形容詞)

2486. The Department of Resources notified the town council that water supply was **contaminated** (polluted).

> 註解　污染 (動詞，被動式)

2487. Doctors prescribe **massive** (heavy) doses of penicillin for patients with pneumonia.

> 註解　大量的 (形容詞)

2488. The ambassador **verified** (confirmed) the report before he called the State Department.

> 註解　證實 (動詞)

2489. The **rivalry** (competition) between the two construction companies was obvious.

> 註解　競爭 (名詞)

2490. The holiday crowds **littered** (dirtied) the park.

> 註解　亂丟垃圾 (動詞)

2491. The automobile's exhaust system **gave off** (emitted) foul-smelling fumes.

> 註解　噴出 (動詞片語)

2492. The camellia is a tree or shrub with **glossy** (shiny) evergreen leaves and waxy, roselike flowers.

> 註解　光滑的 (形容詞)

2493. His qualifications for the graduate assistantship are **indisputable** (unquestionable).

> 註解　沒有疑問的 (形容詞)

2494. The President's greatest **asset** (advantage) was his reputation for honesty.

> 註解　資產 (名詞)

2495. Quito's 9,350-foot elevation makes it the third **loftiest** (highest) capital in the world.

　註解　高的 (形容詞)

2496. The espionage agent agreed not to **divulge** (reveal) the top-secret plans.

　註解　洩露 (不定詞)

2497. The movie critic said that Airplane, the parody of disaster movies, was **hilarious** (very funny).

　註解　有趣的 (形容詞)

2498. The president appears to have been **in earnest** (serious) when he promised to try to balance the national budget.

　註解　真誠的 (形容詞片語)

2499. The **collapse** (failure) of the stock market in 1929 signaled the beginning of the Depression.

　註解　崩潰 (名詞)

2500. The scientist **inspected** (examined) the fossil closely to determine their age.

　註解　檢驗 (動詞)

國家圖書館出版品預行編目資料

托福字彙／李英松編著. ─再版.─新北市：李昭
儀，2020.12
　　冊；　公分.
ISBN 978-957-43-8196-8（上冊：平裝）
1. 托福考試 2. 詞彙
850.1894　　　　　　　　　109016086

托福字彙（上冊）

作　　者　李英松
發 行 人　李英松
出　　版　李昭儀
　　　　　Email：lambtyger@gmail.com
設計編印　白象文化事業有限公司
　　　　　專案主編：林孟侃　　經紀人：洪怡欣
經銷代理　白象文化事業有限公司
　　　　　412台中市大里區科技路1號8樓之2（台中軟體園區）
　　　　　出版專線：（04）2496-5995　　傳真：（04）2496-9901
　　　　　401台中市東區和平街228巷44號（經銷部）
　　　　　購書專線：（04）2220-8589　　傳真：（04）2220-8505
印　　刷　普羅文化股份有限公司
初版一刷　2019 年 5 月初版
　　　　　2019 年 7 月二版
　　　　　2020 年 12 月三版
定　　價　400 元

白象文化　印書小舖 PressStore　出版‧經銷‧宣傳‧設計
www.ElephantWhite.com.tw　f 自費出版的領導者　購書 白象文化生活館